The Girl From Saint Petersburg

Joyana Peters

Always trust your gut!

love
Joyana

To my beautiful children- Owen and Tara
Trust your gut instincts and don't be afraid to take the
occasional leap of faith.

Not like the brazen giant of Greek fame,
With conquering limbs astride from land to land;
Here at our sea-washed, sunset gates shall stand
A mighty woman with a torch, whose flame
Is the imprisoned lightning, and her name
Mother of Exiles. From her beacon-hand
Glows world-wide welcome; her mild eyes command
The air-bridged harbor that twin cities frame.
"Keep, ancient lands, your storied pomp!" cries she
With silent lips. "Give me your tired, your poor,
Your huddled masses yearning to breathe free,
The wretched refuse of your teeming shore.
Send these, the homeless, tempest-tost to me,
I lift my lamp beside the golden door!"
-Emma Lazarus

Would you like a free short story? Sign up for my newsletter at JoyanaPeters.com and get your free short story about the Triangle Shirtwaist Factory Fire!

Follow Me on my Website for more Promos and Giveaway Opportunities!

Chapter One

Chapter One
January 1905--St. Petersburg, Russia

ABRAHAM LEANED FORWARD and slammed his cards down on the kitchen table.

"Rummy! Three in a row."

Ruth sprang to her feet. How could he have won three times in a row? She snatched and checked his cards. "You must have cheated!"

"I did not!" Abraham turned to Ruth's brother. "Jeremiah, defend me here."

"He won fair and square, Ruth," Jeremiah said without glancing up from his book. "And stop dragging me into the middle of your squabbles."

"Not fair," Ruth huffed, throwing down her cards. "You two always gang up on me."

Jeremiah turned a page. "No one likes a sore loser. Keep fussing and Abraham will ask his parents to call off the betrothal. Then he won't want to come over, anymore." He shot her a teasing look. "At least not to see *you*."

Abraham crossed his arms behind his head and leaned back, flashing Ruth a charming smile.

She scowled, her insides a turmoil of confusion—as always when her betrothal to Abraham was mentioned. He was handsome, yes, but sometimes he still seemed more her brother's friend than hers. And he could be so impossible!

As his chair tilted, a card fell onto the floor behind him.

"You did cheat!" Ruth yelled. She scooped up the card and threw it at him.

He laughed and held up his hands in mock surrender.

Jeremiah put aside his book. He jumped from his chair and grabbed Abraham's head under his arm. "How am I supposed to defend you if you make me a liar when I do?"

"Ow, ow. I give up."

"Good. Hope you've learned your lesson." Jeremiah released him and went back to his book.

Abraham picked up his fallen *kippah* and gave Ruth another grin while he secured it back on his head.

He was infuriating! And yet, she could never stay angry at him for long.

There was a knock at the front door and Abraham's expression turned serious.

"That'll be Mark." Jeremiah nudged Abraham. "Time to go."

"Go where?" Ruth asked. "The streets are dangerous these days."

"We have business to take care of. Nothing to concern you." Abraham avoided her eyes.

"What kind of business could you two *putzes* have?"

Abraham puffed out his chest. "Matters concerning the factory. Grown-up affairs."

She glared at him. "Stop treating me like a child. I'm thirteen now. My mother was *married* when she was my age."

He raised his eyebrows, and her face went hot. This time it was Ruth who had brought up marriage. She expected more teasing, but it didn't come. The atmosphere in the room had changed.

"We can't tell you where we're going," Abraham told her. "It's safer you don't know."

"Safer? Why?" Her stomach tightened. "Are you doing something dangerous?"

"Don't worry. We'll tell you when we get back, ya?" Jeremiah leaned in, pecked her cheek and moved toward the door.

"Wait, Jeremiah!"

"What?"

"*Gay ga zinta hate.* Bruder, be careful, promise me." She darted a look at Abraham, who was speaking with Mark in low tones. "Both of you."

"I promise." Jeremiah smiled and winked. "See you later."

He put on his hat, lightly touched the mezuzah and kissed his fingers, before following Abraham and Mark out the door.

As the door closed, Ruth muttered, "Lord, guide their footsteps toward peace. May You rescue them from the hand of every foe and ambush along the way."

Then she crouched to pick the fallen cards from the floor.

Chapter Two

Ruth woke to heavy banging on the front door. Half-asleep, she blinked against the early morning light.

Ester's tousled head shifted on the pillow next to her. "What's happening?"

"I don't know, Bird." Ruth patted her head. "Stay here. I'll find out."

Wincing at the icy floor on her bare feet, she tiptoed out of the bedroom and toward the front door. Her mother was wrapped in her shawl, crouched on the floor and peering over the window sill. Her eyes were puffy and red.

"What are you doing?"

"Shh!" Momme tugged Ruth down beside her. "Don't let them see you."

"Don't let who see us? Where's Tatty? And why were you crying?" Ruth glanced around the house.

Momme clenched Ruth's wrist. "I need you to listen. They'll break in soon. And they will interrogate and hurt me. You need to be brave."

"Interrogate you? I don't understand. Where are Tatty and Jeremiah?"

"Tatty left for America last night, but we can't tell them that."

Ruth shivered. Her father gone to America without saying good-bye? "What? Why? Did Jeremiah go too?"

An odd blankness came over her mother's eyes. She seemed about to answer when an axe crashed through the front door.

"Whatever you do, stay in the bed. Cover yourselves to hide and don't leave Ester." Momme pushed Ruth toward the bedroom.

Ruth scrambled to her feet and ran. She looked back over her shoulder to see her mother standing tall and dusting herself off. As the door gave way and the czar's soldiers invaded the house, her mother's lips moved in silent prayer.

Ruth found her sister hiding under the covers and held a finger to her lips as she crawled in beside her. Ester nodded, suddenly appearing much older than her ten years. As the men's voices rose in the next room, Ruth wrapped her arms around Ester and they lay trembling, tears wetting their shoulders and hair.

There was a slap followed by a muffled sob. Ester cried out. Ruth clapped her hand over Ester's mouth, but a moment later heavy boots stomped toward them and the covers were ripped away.

Two stone-faced soldiers glared down from either side of the bed. They grabbed the girls with rough hands.

"Ruth!" Ester screamed, reaching for her sister.

"She's a child!" Ruth begged. "Please, leave her be."

The soldiers ignored her and dragged the two girls from the house. Ruth looked around for Momme but she had disappeared. The street was in chaos. There were more soldiers, and families shivering in their bed clothes. Why was this happening?

The soldier flung her onto the cold ground, knocking the wind out of her. Gasping, she scrambled toward Ester, but a soldier stepped between them.

"No moving!" he shouted.

"Please, don't hurt us, sir!"

"That depends on your mother. If she tells us what we want to know, we won't need to."

Helplessly, Ruth watched Ester curl up and sob. She tried to squash her instinct to reach for her sister, and instead forced herself to look around for her mother.

And there she was—standing with her chin high, in the middle of four soldiers. Ruth could see a dark splotch on her face. Was it blood? But she remained straight and tall. She wasn't even crying. Ruth was amazed by her mother's control. How did she manage to appear so unaffected?

A soldier with a thick drooping mustache stepped close to Momme.

"Where are they?" he growled in her face.

"I told you, I don't know," she replied.

"I don't believe you." He cracked her on the back of the head with the butt of his rifle and kicked her in the stomach. "Try again. Where are they?"

Momme crumpled forward, coughing. "I don't know."

"This is pointless. Grab the girl." He gestured toward Ester.

The soldier standing near Ester grabbed her and dragged her forward. Ester kicked her legs and thrashed in his arms.

"No!" Momme lurched forward. "Leave her. She

doesn't know anything and neither do I. They never returned home."

"But they *were* in the square yesterday?" the droopy mustache soldier asked.

"Yes."

"What was that? I can't hear you." He cupped his ear.

"Yes, they were there," Momme's voice rang out louder.

Ruth closed her eyes at Momme's words. This was about Abraham and Jeremiah and wherever they had gone yesterday. What trouble had they gotten themselves into? Tatty must have taken them away to America to protect them.

The soldier leaned down into Momme's face. "And the meetings? They attend those, too, don't they?"

Momme turned her head away. He popped her in the forehead with his rifle butt so hard she flew backwards onto the ground. "Answer me!"

A shriek pierced the air from down the street. Ruth saw a man being pulled out of his house. His wife screamed and reached for him, but the soldiers held her back. They forced the man to his knees and one of the soldiers held a pistol to the back of his head. A shot rang out. The man slumped forward.

Ruth looked back at her mother's horror-stricken face. Droopy Mustache grabbed Momme by the hair.

"Perhaps—now you see how serious we are, *drabke*?"

Momme moved her head up and down. "I told you, they never came home. They must be among the dead."

"And the meetings?"

"Yes, they attended them," she croaked. "But if they're dead now, what does it matter?"

He looked at Momme for a long moment. Finally, he let her go and turned to the other soldiers.

"Search the house again."

The soldiers nodded and made their way back into the house. Droopy Mustache remained outside, looming over the girls and Momme, whose gaze was fixed on the house. Ruth heard glass shatter and heavy thumps. Finally, the soldiers returned.

"Nothing," one of them said.

Droopy Mustache nodded and turned back to Momme. "We've closed all roads leaving St. Petersburg. If they're not dead, they will be by the end of the day."

He gestured to his soldiers and led them away. Momme collapsed, and Ruth jumped forward to catch her.

One of Momme's eyebrows trickled blood, and Ruth tried to wipe it away with the sleeve of her nightdress.

"Did they hurt you?" Momme asked Ester.

Ester shook her head. "I'm fine."

"Let's get Momme into the house," Ruth said.

They helped Momme stagger to her feet. Looping her arms around their necks, they half-carried her into the house.

As they settled Momme into the bed, Ruth turned to Ester. "Get some fresh water and rags." Ester nodded and scurried away.

Momme winced as she sank into her pillow. Blood from her eyebrow dribbled onto the pillowcase, freshly laundered yesterday. "You're good girls..."

Ruth sat down next to her. Her stomach tightened, thinking of Jeremiah and Abraham. *If they're not dead, they will be by the end of the day.*

"What happened, Momme?"

Momme sighed and closed her eyes. "I'm too tired..."

"Where are they?"

"Tatty and Abraham left for America. Samuel, too. They should be far enough on their way, I hope."

A chilling realization came to Ruth. Why hadn't Momme mentioned Jeremiah?

"Jeremiah is dead, isn't he?"

Tears pooled in Momme's eyes.

Ruth closed her eyes, trembling—she'd never before felt such a clash of contradictory feelings. Abraham was alive! But her kind-hearted, devoted brother...

Momme turned to her side, facing away from Ruth. Her voice sounded choked when she spoke again. "Could you stoke the fire for hot water? I must wash."

Ruth stood and moved toward the door, her feet heavy, like she was slogging through mud.

"Wait," Momme said. "Don't say anything to Ester yet, about Jeremiah. I'll explain. I just–need time..."

"Yes, Momme."

Ruth closed the door and stepped into the destroyed front room. Standing there among broken glass and plates, toppled furniture and strewn personal belongings, she thought back to last night. The playful teasing, the card game, in this very room.

Just twelve hours ago! The meaning of Momme's words sank in. Jeremiah was dead. She'd never see him again. And Tatty and Abraham, along with Abraham's father, were far away. Did they get out in time? She leaned against the wall. The heat of tears was beginning to burn behind her eyes when she heard Ester's voice, small and wavering. "Where do you want the water, Ruth?"

She wiped her eyes and shook her head to pull herself together.

"Oh, um, we'll need to heat it for Momme. She's still

bleeding. I'll stoke the fire and you get some water for us too."

Ester scurried away. She didn't know about Jeremiah, but Ruth knew she was filled with worry—it was good to give her a task, something to focus on. But Ruth herself could only step into their bedroom and shut the door. She slid down the wall to the floor and allowed her sobs to break free.

Chapter Three

Ruth sighed as she switched the ladle from her right to left hand again. She'd been stirring the simmering stew for the past twenty minutes, hoping it would thicken. There wasn't a speck of flour for sale anywhere. The bakers were all on strike and more vendors would follow. Every time she went out, another shop was closed. The enticing aroma of beef wafted to her nostrils. What if this was the last time they had meat? Her stomach growled at the thought.

A timid knock sounded at the door. Ruth cursed under her breath.

"Ester, can you get the door? I have my hands full here."

Ester scampered to the door with a long trail of yarn from her knitting following her. Ruth rolled her eyes. She pictured another night untangling knots with Ester unable to imagine how they got there.

"Benyamin!" Ester's voice rose an octave in surprise at the sight of Abraham's younger brother. "Since when do you knock?"

Ruth looked over her shoulder to see the boy on the

front stoop shifting his weight from one foot to the other while he kept his gaze on the ground. Something was wrong. She removed the pot from the stove and wiped her hands on her apron as she moved to the door.

"What is it, Benyamin?"

He barely lifted his gaze to meet Ruth's. "My mother wishes to speak to your mother. She sent me to get her."

A chill crept up Ruth's spine. Had Sarah news from the men? Two months had passed since Abraham and his father escaped with Tatty, but there'd been no word since.

Momme left a moment later with Benyamin, giving Ruth a tight-lipped nod. Ruth knew the nod meant she should keep her mouth shut. They didn't want to alarm Ester more than necessary. Ester knew Jeremiah was dead and Tatty had escaped—but as far as she was aware, the family's troubles had ended after the interrogation from the soldiers. Only Ruth and Momme understood how the unpredictable political climate could still affect them.

Ruth returned to the stove and Ester sat down at the table behind her and began winding the trail of yarn.

"Tatty's still in danger, isn't he?"

Ruth winced.

Putting down the yarn, Ester pulled her chair closer. "Tell me the truth, Ruth. We don't actually know he's safe in America yet, do we?"

Ruth weighed her words carefully before answering. "We have not heard confirmation he arrived there, no. But I'm sure they're busy getting settled and the post is slow coming overseas."

She turned to get bowls from the shelf above the counter. As she laid them on the table, she met Ester's concerned look.

"There's no reason to worry, Bird. All is well, I'm sure of it."

"But could that be why Benyamin came to get Momme? Maybe they heard something from Abraham or Samuel?"

Ruth chewed her lower lip as she set the table. At ten, Ester was getting too old to shield.

"That is a possibility, Ester, yes," she admitted.

Ester frowned and got to her feet. "All right, then. Let's eat. We'll save some for Momme."

Ruth nodded before turning to serve the stew. Ducking her face so Ester couldn't see, Ruth wiped a stray tear.

RUTH GLANCED up from her knitting as Momme tiptoed into the house later that night. Ester jumped to her feet and ran to Momme before she'd even unwrapped her shawl.

"Is it Tatty? Did they hear from them?"

Momme shot Ruth a look. Ruth shrugged. "She's putting the pieces together on her own now. There's not much I can do to prevent it."

Momme sighed and hung her shawl on the hook by the door. She then slumped on a kitchen chair. She looked older than her thirty-one years. "Well, it wasn't about Tatty or the men, but it's still bad news. Sarah and the children are leaving."

"Leaving? What do you mean?" Ruth asked.

Momme leaned forward and covered her face with her hands. "Going to Sarah's brother in Bialystok. Their savings are dwindling, and who knows when the men might start sending money? Sarah feels they'll all be better in the country with her brother's family to help."

"You can't stop them?" Ester asked.

"Stop them?" Momme laughed. "How can I blame her? If we had someone to go to, we'd be leaving as well."

Ruth swallowed hard. "When?"

Momme wiped away a tear from her already puffy red eyes. "The end of this week." She got to her feet. "Come, let's go to bed. It's late."

"Aren't you hungry?"

Momme shook her head. "I'm just tired."

As RUTH UNDRESSED for bed she thought of how interwoven the two families had always been. Abraham's father, Samuel, was Tatty's business partner and Sarah was her mother's greatest friend. The betrothal of Abraham and Ruth had only tightened the bonds between all of them. Feeling a surge of anger, Ruth slid her nightgown on and balled her dress in her hand. Momme might not blame Sarah, but Ruth did. Sarah was being selfish. How dare she leave them all behind? How would Momme manage without Sarah to lean on—how would any of them keep going?

Ruth threw her dress to the floor and climbed into bed. She tried to take a few deep breaths to calm herself. Ester already lay curled in a ball on the other side of the bed. How Ester could fall asleep so quickly was a mystery to Ruth. But there she was—already breathing deeply on the brink of snoring. Ruth sighed and turned to her side. She was being unreasonable in her anger toward Sarah. But how could so much change in two months? She was afraid to think what else she might lose.

～

THE END of the week arrived and it was time to say goodbye. Ruth glanced at Momme, who clutched her handkerchief with white knuckles and teetered slightly from side to side, watching the children climb next to their uncle in the cart. Sarah burst into tears as they embraced.

"I'm so sorry, Rachel. You know I wouldn't leave if there was any other way."

"I know." Momme sniffled. "You must protect your family."

Ruth put a hand on Ester's shoulders, trying to lead her away. Was Ester seeing too much? Would she start to question her own safety? Ruth wondered herself what Momme's next move would be. Their own savings were dwindling. What would they do if they didn't hear from Tatty and have money sent from America soon?

Sarah patted Momme on the back one last time and wrenched herself away.

"Make sure you write to us as often as you can," she called as she climbed into the cart.

Momme nodded, still crying too hard to speak. Then the cart pulled away and they were left standing alone. Momme wiped her eyes and took a few deep breaths before turning back to the girls.

"I guess that's it, then. We'd best start dinner." She opened the front door and gestured for them to follow.

～

TWO WEEKS LATER, Ruth was sitting at the table, sewing, when a knock rattled the door.

"Mail Delivery!"

Ruth ran across the room. The post man smiled and tipped his hat.

"Must be exciting to hear from family in America, ya?"

Ruth nodded and closed the door. Her eyes scanned the envelope as she made her way to the back garden to find Momme. The postmarks were strange, but the beloved handwriting was Tatty's. Then her gaze fell on the return address on the back. Uncle Avi? Who was that?

Momme was clipping a sheet to the clothesline. She froze when she saw Ruth holding the envelope.

"Is that...?"

Ruth shook her head. "I don't understand. It's Tatty's writing, but the return address reads Uncle Avi. We don't know anyone by that name."

Momme rushed to grab the envelope from Ruth's hand.

"That's your father's code so the czar's censors won't know who sent it!"

"Oh." Ruth's stomach dropped. The czar's soldiers were still looking for the participants from the rally last January, but she hadn't imagined they would read their mail. Could the czar's control really extend to America? Or was Tatty worried about putting *them* in danger for their connection to him? The memory of Momme surrounded by the soldiers flickered back to her.

Momme tore open the letter. Her mouth formed the words as she read silently to herself, as if trying to commit them to memory. Tears streamed down her face. Ruth took a step closer, but then stopped. Through Momme's tears, she was smiling. She was more at peace than Ruth had seen her since Tatty left. Ruth slipped back inside to allow Momme to enjoy this moment alone with her husband.

Three days later another letter arrived, this time addressed to Ruth from "Cousin David." Abraham! Her heart fluttered. She tore open the envelope, prepared to read words of reassurance and promises about their future reunion. Instead, she found:

Dearest Cousin,

We have settled into this bustling city called New York and found work. I have never seen such tall buildings or so many people. It makes St. Petersburg look like a small dorf or shtetl. It will take time to grow accustomed. Cousin Jacob's spirit and creative ambition would be helpful and are missed every day as I attempt to find my place in this new world.

New York also has fewer trees. Nothing like the beautiful tree at the end of the market street. Remember the day we climbed to the top and carved our names on the highest branch we could reach? Things were much simpler then.

I hope you are in good health as well as your mother and sister. I'll write again soon with more details about my time here.

Shalom,
Cousin David

RUTH THREW the letter down on the table. After so much time apart, did Abraham really have no emotions to share? I hope you are in good health. Could he be more formal? It truly felt like he was speaking to a distant relative instead of the girl he was meant to marry.

Momme crossed the room and picked up the letter from the table and handed it back to Ruth.

"You have to read between the lines, Ruth," she said with a smile. "They know the letters are being read by the czar's people."

At first Ruth didn't understand what Momme meant by reading between the lines. But after re-reading Abraham's letter dozens of times, she finally saw the deeper meaning.

The carving in the tree ——she'd honestly thought he'd forgotten about that day. He'd never mentioned it afterward. But reading the words brought the memory back.

She closed her eyes for a moment, remembering the magnificent tree, how the leaves had shifted against the sky.

They'd been surprised to discover such a massive tree in the city. She hadn't wanted to climb it, not at first—in fact, it scared her to see how nine-year-old Abraham's eyes shone as he gazed up.

"It's perfect," Abraham had said. "Let's do it."

Ruth was already tired from keeping up with the boys all morning. That *fershtinkiner,* Abraham, was always wanting the biggest challenge he could find! And her foolish brother could never refuse.

"Wait, Jeremiah." Ruth pulled him back by the arm. "You're not actually considering this?"

Jeremiah shrugged. "Why not?"

"Because it's a *fercockt* challenge! That tree is gigantic. You could fall and kill yourself!"

"Any challenge has risk," Abraham said. "But if you want to turn into a girl on us, run along home to the kitchen. Just don't be a tell-tale."

He turned back to the tree and began assessing his approach, pulling down on the nearest branches to gauge the weight they'd hold.

Jeremiah put his hand on Ruth's arm. "You can stay down and watch. I'll not think less of ya. No one expects you to always keep up with us." He mussed her hair and she swatted away his hand. He ran toward the tree. She stuck her tongue out at his back. Stupid boys. Not think less of her? She was the only one thinking reasonably.

But as the boys swung into the monstrous tree and began their ascent, Ruth shifted her weight from one foot to the other. There'd be such freedom and satisfaction in completing such a challenge. She thought of the chopping and peeling and other chores waiting for her in the kitchen if she went home.

Before logic overtook her again, she took off running toward the tree and seized the nearest branch. Her muscles screamed as she pulled herself up and leaves scratched at her face and clung to her hair. Only when she was mostly up did she make the mistake of looking down.

It was Abraham who came back to help her. First, he sat on the branch next to hers and carved her name with his knife so she could say she completed the challenge. Then he carved his own.

"Don't you want to carve it at the top with Jeremiah?"

"I'd rather celebrate how far you made it. I should learn to stop doubting, because you always prove me wrong," he said with a smile. "Now follow my lead as I chart our path down. I'll go first so you know I'm there to catch you."

As he began the climb back down, Ruth noticed he'd left his knife sitting in the crook of the branch. She picked it up and gently carved a faint heart around their two names. She knew at that moment he'd be hers and would always be. After tucking the knife into the pocket of her skirt, she followed him down, her fear completely dissipated.

HAD Abraham gone back to the tree and seen the heart? Or was he just remembering the special moment they'd shared? For her, that had been the turning point in their relationship. The day they'd evolved from annoying "siblings" sharing nothing more than Jeremiah, to a boy and a girl who actually saw each other. It was true there were times he still seemed like no more than her brother's infuriating friend—especially when she caught him cheating at cards—yet the feeling that had begun at the tree never went away completely. That was why when, years later, her parents had told her of the betrothal, it had both surprised her and seemed completely natural.

She clutched the letter to her chest as new understanding resonated through. Apparently, he treasured the memory of the tree as she did. So, this letter was actually a precious love letter.

She pulled out paper and sat down at the kitchen table to write back. Momme put a hand on her shoulder.

"You can't tell him how bad things are here."

"I know, because of the censorship." Ruth nodded and dipped her pen in ink. "I'll find a way to put it in code."

"No," Momme said. "We need them to believe all is well."

Ruth stared at her mother in shock. "You want me to lie?"

Momme sighed. "I want you to protect them. They can't change anything for us from there. Why worry them?"

"So we suffer without even being able to tell them?"

Momme nodded and stroked Ruth's head. "That's the burden we must bear."

Ruth avoided any references to her life at all. It was easier than lying directly.

As time went on, she filled her letters with memories of better times, or asked follow-up questions to details Abraham included about his exciting new life. Was learning English difficult? What was it like to attend a movie? An intimate shorthand developed and Ruth grew to rely on his letters to help her soldier on as the months dragged slowly by and the city grew angrier and more desperate.

Chapter Four

Evening was fast descending. Ruth cursed the shortening daylight hours—autumn was turning to winter, and she'd soon have to adjust her marketing time to get it in before curfew. The chill in the air made Ruth's nose run. She wiped it with her sleeve and quickened her pace. She rounded the corner from the marketplace and felt the impact of a woman's bony frame crashing into her, sending her groceries tumbling.

"Watch where you're going!"

"Sorry," Ruth mumbled. She scrambled to gather her groceries, but wasn't quick enough.

The disheveled woman swiped a rotting cabbage and stuck it under her filthy cape before skittering away. Ruth sighed. So much for cabbage soup tonight. The woman had collided with her on purpose. It was a trick she herself was increasingly tempted to try, if she didn't think Momme would somehow find out—and kill her. Momme swore they'd never be desperate enough to let go of their morals. Ruth wasn't so sure. These were miserable times and everyone was fighting to survive.

As Ruth continued her way home, two men stumbled into her path from one of the taverns. She shrank back, hoping they wouldn't notice her, a lone woman out at dusk. Now she was seventeen, she supposed she qualified as a woman in their eyes—at times like this, she regretted the extra attention her maturity brought her.

She followed at a careful distance, cursing their meandering pace. The sky was darkening fast. One of the drunken men clapped a hand on his friend's shoulder.

"Pyotr, mark my words, three weeks, tops! With the railroad on board, the country's at a standstill. The czar will yield."

"No, no." The friend slapped the first man's hand from his shoulder and held up his own hand to count off on fingers. "No railroad, no mail, no newspapers. He's got nothing. I say he rolls over in a few days! He'll beg a parliament to form."

Ruth rolled her eyes. She was so sick of the revolution and this stupid strike. It was overconfident boasts like these that ignited the chaos nine months ago. The protestors believed from the first they could force the czar's hand. Instead, they were met with guns and bullets, or forced into exile like Abraham and Tatty. But still the delusions continued!

Each time another business joined the country-wide strike everyone got stirred up again, and declared the czar would give in. As far as she saw it, they were two months into this strike, and the only results were starvation, poverty and illness, while the czar remained snug in his palace unmoved. Ruth wanted to believe in the cause that had robbed her of her brother and forced her father and Abraham into hiding. But each day it grew harder to remain strong. She was hungry and tired.

A cat scurried out in front of her, knocking over half a tower of wooden crates. Ruth ducked behind the remaining crates, heart pounding.

"What was that?" one of the men said.

Had they seen her? She heard them laugh as they realized they'd been startled by a cat.

"Make enough noise to wake the giants, eh, you stinking cat?" The echo of the men's laughter faded as they continued on their way.

Ruth's breathing steadied, and she peeped from her hiding place. The street was desolate, except for the cat, who sat casually licking one paw. Ruth took off running—curfew would go into effect any moment. She began to pant and her side throbbed with a cramp. But she continued running until she turned into the alley by her house and collapsed against the wall to catch her breath. She couldn't let Momme and Ester see her like this. As she gasped, she was hit with the stench of the ever-growing garbage piles lining the street. Because of the strike, no one had come to collect it in weeks.

She pushed off the wall and continued past her neighbors' once-tidy little homes, now in disrepair. Some, thanks to the soldiers, were nothing but piles of ash. She glimpsed the house Abraham and his family had lived in. It visibly sagged, its shutters askew, and made her miss them even more. There were times she almost forgot they were gone. She'd think to head over there to ask a question or borrow something, only to realize all over again. Then the loneliness kicked in.

Ester was waiting for Ruth outside, plopped on the front stoop with her gangly legs stretched in front of her. She clapped her hands in excitement when she saw Ruth. "You're home! Did you get bread?"

Ruth rolled her eyes. "The bakers aren't making any, remember?"

Ester pursed her lips in a pout. "Is it a crime to hope?"

"You can hope, but they seem to be holding on to the idea of no vote, no bread."

Ester stood, hunching her shoulders. "You don't need to bite my head off for asking. Why are you in such a bad mood?"

Not wanting to confess to losing the cabbage, Ruth deflected. "Why are you sitting outside?"

Ester looked down to the ground. "I needed a break. Momme's grumpy, too— it's been a rough day."

"So you left her?" Ruth scowled at her sister. Yes, Momme had been difficult lately, snapping and crying in turn. But hiding outside to avoid her? Ruth couldn't condone that cowardice. She pushed past Ester and stepped inside.

Ruth had never seen their home so chaotic. The table was covered with a jumble of items. Drawers were open, spilling their contents. The wall decorations—papercuts and Momme's favorite calligraphy—were scattered across the sofa. Had Momme finally lost her mind?

As Ruth pondered the situation, Momme bustled into the kitchen.

"Good you're here. You can help."

"Help with what?" Ruth asked hesitantly.

Momme picked up a brass candlestick and polished it with her apron. "The money's gone, Ruth. We have nothing left."

Ruth's thoughts whirled. Gone? It had been two months and eight days since she'd last received a letter from Abraham. That would also have been the last time Momme had received any cash from Tatty. No wonder she was frantic.

"What are we going to do?" Ruth asked.

Momme gestured to the crowded table. "Find money ourselves."

"You want to sell our stuff?"

Momme shrugged. "What choice do we have?"

Ruth looked around the haphazard piles. Each item held significance to the family— the hand-carved chess set Tatty and Jeremiah had loved, the candlesticks that held their prayer candles for the high holidays. She understood Momme's logic and knew she was right. But how could they part with these memories?

"I think I've gathered everything," Momme said in a cold voice devoid of emotion. "Now help me organize so we can be strategic."

Ruth nodded. They began organizing objects by value and by how desperate they would need to be to sell them. Ester watched them with a frown.

"Momme, you're not selling your wedding ring, are you?"

Momme paused from sorting her jewelry box. "Not yet, *sheifele*."

"Then why is it in the pile?" Ester asked, jutting her chin to point.

Momme sighed. "Because it's gold. And if it comes to a choice between survival or the ring, I'll have to let it go."

She reached for Ester's hand as Ester's eyes filled with tears. "But that's my last choice pile, Bird. I hope we never use them."

Ruth looked to the two items in Momme's "last choice" pile. Ruth recognized the wedding ring of course, but she'd never seen the other piece. It was an intricate gold brooch with emerald gem stones.

Ruth reached for the piece. "Where did you get this?"

Momme snatched the brooch away. "It was my mother's."

Ruth recognized her tone— the "Don't ask another question" tone. Momme never spoke about her parents or sisters. Tatty explained once she had lost them in a traumatic way.

Momme slipped the brooch back into a suede pouch and returned it to her jewelry box. She then picked up a set of candlesticks and handed them to Ruth.

"Start polishing. The more they gleam, the more they'll bring."

RUTH SET out at daybreak with the candlesticks, determined not to return until she had sold them. She wandered from shop to shop for hours. A few shopkeepers pointed to already overflowing piles of objects provided by others in the same position. Some offered store credit. Finally, she found someone willing to buy the candlesticks and count out cash into her outstretched hand.

She came home waving the cash in the air to celebrate.

"That's all you got?" Momme asked.

Ruth's stomach dropped. "They're overrun with people doing the same."

Momme counted the bills. "This will barely buy coal and groceries for the week."

It became a weekly routine. Momme selected an item from the pile. She'd polish it until it gleamed, gritting her teeth the entire time. Then Ruth would sell it and stick the money into the jar on the shelf. Ruth got better at haggling, questioning the offering until an extra ruble or two was added to the pile. But as the strike rolled into the third month, fewer and fewer shops pulled out cash at all. And soon the jar was empty.

Chapter Five

The room was pitch black. They'd been going to bed right after sunset to conserve oil and coal—, and slept all bundled together in Momme's bed for warmth. At first it was strange, another sign of the danger they were in. But over time, going to bed so early and sitting in the dark had become Ruth's favorite part of the day. Momme would pass the time telling stories. Cuddled next to Momme and her sister, Ruth felt almost peaceful.

One night, Momme was in the middle of a favorite folktale from her childhood about a boy and a goat, when they heard cheers in the street. They sprang out of bed and ran to the window. Their few remaining neighbors stood in the street hugging and laughing while others carried tables and chairs from their houses. Mrs. Abramovich and Mrs. Aleshkovsky from down the block walked around with trays of glasses while their husbands followed, pouring from bottles of vodka. Momme took her shawl and ran out the front door with the girls quick on her heels.

"What has happened?" Momme asked grabbing Mrs. Abramovich by the arm.

"The czar agreed to a parliament. He's giving us a voice!"

"Does that mean—"

"The strike is over!" Old Man Lashevich from across the street smiled. "Still a long road to go. Knowing the czar, he'll change his mind again. But tonight, we celebrate."

Someone picked up a violin and began to play. Soon he was joined by a harmonica and two boys banging on overturned trash pails. Dancers flocked to the area in front of the makeshift band.

Ruth watched Momme survey the happy scene in wonder. Then Momme shrugged off her shawl, grabbed Ruth and Ester by the hands and twirled them into the crowd. Ruth felt the cool night air on her face and laughed as she saw Momme tilt her head back in joy. The deep worry lines on Momme's face seemed to disappear. Ruth felt the tension in her own shoulders ease. They hiked up their skirts and danced as if for one night they didn't have a care in the world.

The following morning Ruth rose before Momme and Ester. She looked at their peaceful forms splayed in sleep, hair spilling over the pillows, and tiptoed from the room. In the kitchen, she peeked out the window to see the remnants of the celebration the night before strewn throughout the street. What a night it had been! They'd danced and sung till almost dawn, only climbing into bed as fingertips of sunlight crept around the houses. No wonder Momme and Ester were still sound asleep. Ruth wished she could be as well. Yet, a tiny niggle of fear was starting to form.

Momme declared all would be better now. The mail would start again. Tatty's letters and money would arrive and they would be saved. But Mr. Lashevich's words echoed in Ruth's mind. "Knowing the czar, he'll change his mind again." What if Lashevich was right? What if they were prematurely celebrating? It had happened before, the czar going back on his word.

Ruth started to calculate in her head. What if they had only a few months of reprieve before things shut down again? How much money could come through from Tatty during that time? They needed a cushion of savings again. They needed an income. But how?

By the time Momme stumbled into the kitchen an hour later, Ruth had the hatchings of a plan. She waited eagerly as Momme prepared herself a cup of tea with the pot of hot water Ruth had left warming and sat down across from her at the table.

"I have an idea."

Momme sighed and rubbed her face. "For what exactly?"

Ruth's excitement dimmed. Maybe this wasn't the right time to broach her plan. Momme appeared more tired than Ruth had anticipated. Ruth waited another moment until Momme gestured for her to go on.

She took a deep breath. "We need steady income. So, I'm thinking I should get a job."

Momme's cup froze halfway to her mouth. "Why would you possibly be thinking that?"

She put down her tea, which sloshed onto the table.

"I don't trust the czar," Ruth said. "I fear he'll go back on his word. Then what? We'll be in the same position we were. With no savings to speak of."

Momme's eyes clouded over. "What about Tatty's money?"

"What of it, Momme?" Ruth leaned forward in her chair. "If the mail stops again, it will stop, too."

"We could ask him to send extra in the meantime, just in case."

"You think he has extra?" Ruth shook her head. "No, we cannot rely on the mail as our only source of income. We must protect ourselves."

Momme stared into her tea cup and said nothing. Had she heard anything Ruth had said? Was she angry? Was she sad? Ruth scowled in irritation, but managed to hold her tongue as she waited for Momme's response.

Momme wet her lips before speaking. "What kind of job would you get?"

Ruth shrugged. "I don't know. Maybe a factory job? I hadn't really thought that far."

Momme ran her fingertip around the edge of her teacup. "I could try taking in some washing and sewing as well."

Ruth nodded. "Good. And Ester could help you."

Momme looked up sharply. "When she gets home from school. She *must* return to school."

"Of course!" Ruth smiled. "I also listened to Tatty's lectures about education over the years. Could probably recite them in my sleep."

Momme gave a small laugh. "*An education is the key to unlocking the future. Reading unlocks doors to anything and everything...*"

Ruth reached across the table and covered Momme's hand with her own. "We'll honor his wishes as best we can."

Momme's eyes glistened. "Things really will never be the same, will they?"

Before Ruth could answer, Ester came bustling into the kitchen.

"What are you two looking so mopey for? Aren't we supposed to be celebrating?"

Ruth jumped from the table and put her arm around her sister. "Yes, Bird, we are. Let's get breakfast going."

Ruth glanced back to see Momme wiping her eyes. Once again, she appeared hunched with the weight of the world on her shoulders. Ruth hated herself for bringing the tension back to Momme. She'd bring back the carefree, dancing Momme. She'd fix this. She'd start looking for a job first thing tomorrow.

She squeezed Ester's shoulder and smiled at her sister.

Today she'd celebrate.

Chapter Six

"We only speak Russian here, none of that Yiddish nonsense," the foreman said, sliding his gaze over Ruth from head to toe. Her eyes strayed to the scarves she'd laid out on his desk. Her best work to impress him. Would it work?

He examined the scarves and pinched one between his fingers. "You stitched all of these?"

Ruth nodded, afraid to speak. Her Russian was mediocre. She only ever used it in school or when absolutely necessary.

He picked up a scarf and examined the gold flowered edge. It was impeccable work. Momme had been drilling Ester and Ruth in embroidery technique since they could hold a needle.

"These are by hand." He put the scarf back on the desk. "Do you know how to use the Singer machine?"

Ruth shook her head, her worst fears realized. The Singer machines were taking over the factories, the whole country! The Singer headquarters were right outside St. Petersburg. Salesmen had fanned out through all but the poorest of neighborhoods. They had come to the door more than once, trying to persuade Momme to buy a machine on installments of only one ruble a week. Like they had even *that* much to spare! Momme was adamant that even if she did buy a machine someday, she would never trust it to do fine work–"Technique will always outweigh efficiency."

The foreman sighed and drummed his fingers on his desk. "I'll see if a girl can train you. But only because a girl just quit and we need the spot filled immediately. You have one day. If you can't pick it up–that's it. I can't have output time wasted."

Ruth's mouth felt like cotton and she swallowed to speak. "Thank you, sir." She hurriedly gathered her scarves and followed as he escorted her to the floor. He stopped before an empty seat at one of the tables and gestured to the girl sitting next to it. "You, teach her the machine."

He disappeared before the girl could respond.

Ruth sat down and turned to the girl with a tentative smile–unable to gauge her reaction. Did the girl resent having her day taken over by a trainee? Her face remained impassive as she concentrated on finishing the stitching on the scarf in her machine.

Ruth felt her body tilting closer to see the beautiful design taking shape. It was a bright blue explosion of swirls and flowers. Right there, Ruth was converted. No way could Momme's precise stitching, expert as it was, compete with what was coming out of that machine. It would have taken months to accomplish what this girl did in minutes.

The girl repeated the swirls and flowers around the entire edge of the scarf, as Ruth craned her neck to watch. Finally, the girl looked up and smiled triumphantly.

"Ready to try yourself?" she asked as she folded the finished scarf.

"Me?" Ruth sputtered.

The girl laughed. She placed the folded scarf into a basket. "That's why you're here, isn't it?"

Ruth straightened her shoulders and nodded. It was. Despite the fluttering in her stomach, she was a capable seamstress. And her family needed her to keep this job. So, yes, she was ready to try.

"I'm Riva," the girl said.

"Ruth."

Riva leaned in and whispered, "Are you more comfortable with Yiddish?"

Ruth nodded, relieved. "Is it allowed?"

Riva winked and responded in Yiddish. "Just between us. Let's get you going then, Ruth." She loaded thread in the machine and grabbed a new scarf from the stack. "See the pattern in pencil on the scarf? Follow along and guide the fabric through. It's easier than it seems."

She demonstrated how to pump the pedals with her foot and watched as Ruth muddled through a scarf on her own. It was a mess, but each scarf got better. With Riva cheering her on and giving her helpful feedback, Ruth's confidence grew. She could do this. Still, her stomach clenched as the foreman reviewed her work at the end of the day.

"Could be better," he said with a shrug. "But good enough."

As he moved on to another station, Ruth felt her eyes well up.

"I have the job," she whispered.

Riva smiled and squeezed her arm. "You earned the job."

Months passed in a blur. Riva and Ruth became fast friends. The factory itself was a soul-sucking, joyless environment. Their hours were long. Few breaks were offered and the pay was horrific. All the same, Ruth felt pride and security as she walked home each week with ruble notes tucked in her pocket. Momme had set a jar on the top shelf in the kitchen where they both contributed their pay. Momme's time was quickly getting booked with embroidery requests and washing jobs. Things were looking up. Until they weren't.

Almost a year had passed since Czar Nicholas had agreed to the formation of the Duma. Elections had occurred, although few were allowed to vote in them. But one warm and rainy evening, Ruth stepped out of the factory to chaos on the street. A mob surrounded two guards, taunting and shoving them. Horrified by the guards' white faces, Ruth took off at a run, away from the scene toward home. But everywhere she looked, angry people shouted and waved their fists. A glass bottle flew above her head and shattered on the building behind her. Her throat filled with fear. Why was this happening? Would she make it home?

She weaved through the hordes, ducking her head and trying not to attract notice. The usual ten-minute walk took an agonizing half hour. She almost cried with relief when she turned onto her block and her house came into view. She sprinted the last few feet and banged open the door.

Momme flew from the kitchen table and wrapped Ruth in a tight, shawled embrace. Ester hugged her from the other side. Ruth finally felt safe. But as they pulled apart, she noticed Momme's puffy eyes and tear-streaked cheeks.

"What happened?" Ruth asked. "It's like the city's gone crazy."

Momme pulled out her handkerchief and wiped her nose. "The czar disbanded the Duma."

Ruth sucked in a breath. "But why?"

Momme shrugged. "He didn't like what they had to say. Who knows? I'm sure he has his reasons."

Momme always tried to defend the czar. But Ruth felt a chill creep up her spine and wrapped her arms around herself. "This is going to get really ugly."

At that, Momme nodded.

The next few days were even worse. Ruth skittered through the street trying to avoid trouble. She was afraid to go out, but more afraid to stay home–the foreman had threatened to give away the job of anyone who didn't show. As she worked, she bent her head, trying to ignore the angry shouts outside and the reflection of fires through the windows.

One evening, Ruth and Momme stayed up later than usual. Ruth sat at the table writing to Abraham, struggling to find words that wouldn't reveal the extent of their hardships. Ester had fallen asleep next to Momme on the sofa.

Momme glanced at the barricaded front door and put down the embroidered scarf she'd been stitching.

She sighed. "I don't know why I bother. My clients are gone."

"What do you mean?" Ruth asked.

"They're gone, either killed or fled the city if they're smart. But either way, no one will be coming to me for washing or stitching. Not while this is going on."

Ruth glanced at the metal jar on the shelf, chewing her lower lip. Things had been going so well, they'd gotten cocky. They'd been sure it was only a matter of time before they saved enough for passage to America. The czar–everything was always about the czar! Their own little family would never be left alone. Even their hopes and dreams could not be their own.

Her mind whirled with what might lay ahead. More strikes? The mail shut down again? They had to protect themselves. They couldn't just wait to see what happened. They had to *act*.

"Momme, I think we need to pull Ester from school and get her working."

"What purpose would pulling her out of school serve? She can't bring me more jobs."

"She can come and work with me at the factory."

Momme shuddered. "She is only twelve! I will not have her locked up in a factory all day. Besides, what good would it do us?"

Twelve. Ruth looked at her sister sleeping peacefully, her tousled head resting near Momme's shoulder. Ruth's insides shrank at what she was condemning her poor sister to. Yet, plenty of others were doing the same. And what choice did they have?

"It would be another income," Ruth said. "Something between us and starvation when prices for food go up again and the mail gets delayed."

"We don't know that will happen–" Momme's voice shook. "We can try to sell more things——"

"As everyone will be trying." Ruth pressed her lips together.

"We don't even know the factories will stay open," Momme argued.

"All the more reason Ester should start now."

Momme didn't reply. Ruth knew she'd won the argument. She didn't feel triumphant, though.

Ruth got to her feet with a scrape of her chair. "I'm going to bed." She couldn't bear to stay in the room another minute–Momme's black despair seemed to fill the air.

Momme wouldn't even look at her. As Ruth left the

room, she saw Momme gently kiss Ester's forehead. Was she being a monster, doing this to Ester?

Ruth bit her lip. Why was she the one making the hard choices? She hated making Ester quit school as much as Momme did. But, there was no choice. And she'd feel worse if she didn't fight for their survival.

Chapter Seven

The cold breeze whipped through the street and cut like a knife to the bone. Ruth pulled her threadbare coat tighter. Next to her, Ester staggered, like the wind might literally knock her over.

Ester burst into a fresh bout of coughing. She'd been coughing for days, but now it seemed to wrack her whole body. It woke her at night and disrupted her work at the factory. Ruth was covering Ester's pile as well as her own to get them through quota.

Ester leaned against a building to steady herself as she coughed. Ruth rubbed her back, but it didn't do much good through her coat. Ruth hated feeling so helpless. What could she do for her sister? Tea with thyme and honey when they got home? She'd already been packing Ester in with hot water bottles and blankets every night. She'd love to get her hands on some goose grease for Ester's chest, but that was impossible these days. Maybe one of those black-market vendors? But how much would they charge?

"Ruth?" Ester's voice sounded panicked. She showed Ruth her mittened hands where she'd coughed up a big wad of mucous and blood. Ruth's stomach dropped. Blood was bad. Blood meant consumption.

She patted Ester's shoulder and tried to smile."That's nothing, Bird. You've been coughing too long and your throat is raw."

Ester eyed Ruth, skepticism and fear in her big brown eyes.

"I promise, you have nothing to fear." The lie tasted like sawdust on Ruth's tongue.

She put an arm around Ester's shoulders and they continued on their way, stopping twice more for coughing fits. Finally, the house was in sight. As always, Ruth was comforted, but of course there was no magic at home. Yes, she could tuck Ester into bed and make her comfortable. But then what? What would home solve if it was consumption?

Momme jumped from the table to greet them. Her face paled when she took in Ester's bloody hands and the spittle clinging to her lips. But she calmly told Ruth to prepare a hot water bottle and tea, and led Ester to bed.

When Ruth joined them there, she found Momme rubbing her sister's feet with peppermint oil.

Ruth placed the tea on the table next to the bed and slipped the water bottle between the sheets. Ester was already asleep.

"She feels hot," Momme said.

"Feverish?"

Momme nodded. "I'm afraid, Ruth."

Ruth's stomach churned. Ester's illness was her fault. She'd pushed for Ester to work in the factory. The awful hours wore her down. She'd overpowered Momme and taken over as head of the household and now look where they were.

Swallowing her panic, she tried to think rationally.

"We need to get the doctor."

Momme's eyes grew wide. "How? We can't afford it."

"We have to. I'll bring what we have and beg. I'll make him come." Ruth put an awkward hand on Momme, who was hunched form over Ester on the bed.

"It'll be okay."

Momme gave a short nod and poured more peppermint oil into her hand. Ruth left the room and went to the money jar. Even after months of saving every penny from her and Ester's salaries and Tatty's letters, it was only half full. Ruth tried to ignore the dangerous thought of what would happen if they used it all. Because what would happen if they didn't?

She emptied the jar and stuffed its contents into her pockets. Then she picked up the wraps she'd discarded only minutes before, and bundled herself once again against the cold. It was close to curfew. The idea of being out on the streets after dark made her uneasy. What if she got robbed before she could get the doctor? She adjusted her scarf with trembling hands, then opened the door and took off running to the doctor's house.

Ruth couldn't remember the last time she'd been to this side of the city. Since beginning work, she barely went anywhere except the factory. Hurrying through the residential neighborhood, she saw broken windows and doors. Some houses were reduced to piles of ashes. The devastation seemed starker than in the industrial area where the factory was.

What was most startling were the smaller houses, similar to Ruth's own that were now abandoned. Many people, like Abraham's family, had fled. And others... Well, everyone knew the persecution and mysterious disappearances of Jews was happening again.

She remembered Riva, who had been so kind, showing her how to use the sewing machine. The memory of Riva's gentle face was like a stab in her gut. The morning of Ester's first day of work, Ruth had chattered all the way to the factory about her new mentor and friend.

"Wait till you see how fast she can finish a pattern and how meticulous her stiches are! She'll teach you everything, just like she taught me."

Ester nodded, and by the time they reached the factory she was even smiling. They climbed the long staircase and bustled into the busy room. But when they reached Riva's station, her chair was empty. She never appeared, and Ruth never saw her again. According to rumor, Riva and her family had been taken away to the Pale of Settlement in the middle of the night.

Ruth noticed the light shifting behind the houses. The sun was almost gone. She had no time to think of Riva—she had to focus on her sister right now. Spotting the doctor's house, she quickened her step and mentally rehearsed her request.

She banged on the doctor's door.

It opened a crack.

"My sister is dying. It's an emergency," she said.

A man with slicked-back greasy hair looked her up and down. "Do you have money?"

"Almost thirty rubles."

He tsked and began to shut the door. But Ruth's desperation turned to fury. She jammed her foot into the opening, and then pushed past him into the house.

"You turn away good money? It's an emergency. You have to help!"

"Everything is an emergency now." The doctor picked up a bottle from the table and poured himself a drink. "People are dying all over the city."

"That doesn't mean you can turn them away and ignore them," Ruth cried. "You're a doctor. You need to try to help."

He shrugged. "I can't be five places at once. There has to be some way to weed people out. Money's as good as any."

As he raised the glass to his mouth, Ruth noticed a spatter of blood marking the cuff of his sleeve. Remnants of grease from his supper clung to his beard and his graying white shirt stretched so tight across his pot-belly, the buttons to pulled in the button-holes.

"You disgust me," she said bitterly.

He chuckled. "A fiery one, I like it."

She turned away.

"Maybe, we can work out an arrangement after all," he said.

Ruth paused, one hand on the door. "What kind of arrangement?"

His hand traveled down to his belt and he began unbuckling his trousers. "There are other kinds of payment, my dear."

She tasted vomit at the back of her mouth. How dare he? He was supposed to be a healer!

He moved closer and heat rose from her chest. Red spots appeared before her eyes. She darted away, grabbing the vodka bottle from the table.

Waving the vodka bottle wildly as she flew, she felt it connect with his head. She saw the surprise on his face as his arms cartwheeled behind him. Suddenly, Ruth was on top of him. He lay beneath her on the ground. She raised the broken bottle to hit him again, but saw the blood on his face, the pool forming beneath his head. He wasn't moving. She lowered the bottle and staggered. Was he dead? Had she killed him?

All the heat trickled from her body, replaced by cold—like there was an ice block in her stomach.

Her mind spun. Who knew she was here? Momme. Had anyone seen her knock at the door? She looked for a trash bucket to get rid of the bottle, and dropped it with a clink on the other bottles already there. She then pulled out her handkerchief and shakingly wiped the blood from her hands and her dress as best she could.

She glanced around the room, trying to spot more traces she may have left behind. Her gaze fell on the doctor's black leather medicine bag on the table. Ester. She still needed to help Ester.

Before she could talk herself out of it, she grabbed the bag and dashed for the door.

Ruth ran through the dark streets as fast as her legs could carry her, clutching the medicine bag like a baby. Her heart raced in her chest. If anyone spotted her, she was finished. Anyone she'd meet after curfew would probably kill for the bag's contents and any soldier would arrest her on the spot.

A flash of light and voices ahead stopped her in her tracks. She flattened herself against the wall, panting and praying. A mob of about ten men holding torches thundered past. Their raucous laughter sent chills through Ruth's body. What damage would they be imposing tonight? Another house burning? Another beating or...

In her mind, she saw the prone body of the doctor on the floor, in the spreading puddle of blood. Was she no better than these mobs of men now? She staggered, the medicine bag suddenly heavy in her arms. Like her guilt added extra weight.

As the voices of the men moved out of earshot, Ruth tightened her grip on the bag and increased the pace of her weary legs. Guilt served no purpose. There was no time for a conscience now. She had done what she needed to do. The only thing to worry about was getting back to help Ester.

She streaked though the streets like a shadow warrior. She made it home in record time and burst through the door. Momme called out to her from the bedroom. What would she say to Momme? She couldn't tell her what had really happened–no, that secret she would carry to the grave. But how would she explain the medicine bag?

She dropped the bag on the floor and rummaged through it frantically. Instruments. Scalpels. Glass bottles. She pulled a bottle from the bottom. White pills rattled around inside. What were they? She heard Momme call out to her again. Pocketing the pill bottle, she tucked the bag behind the stove.

Ruth hurried to the bedroom, which was dark except for a candle by Ester's bedside. Ester's face looked as white as the pillow she lay upon, her hair splayed around her like a dark halo. Her forehead shimmered with sweat.

Momme sat in a chair next to the bed, stroking Ester's hand. "Her fever's worse."

"Did you sponge her down with a cool rag?"

"Of course! It's the first thing I did when she felt warm."

Ruth sighed. She and Momme were always second-guessing each other these days. It almost felt like they were competing about who knew best.

Ruth's voice cracked. "The doctor couldn't come."

Momme's posture deflated. The last bit of hope seemed to drain from her eyes.

Ruth reached for Momme's shoulder. "Why don't you try making some soup? Tatty always said your soup had magical properties."

A tiny smile flickered across Momme's face. "He did, didn't he?"

Ruth nodded and helped Momme to her feet. She waited until she heard Momme rattling pots and bowls in the kitchen before reaching into her pocket.

She had no idea what the pills were or what they'd do. But Ester looked so ill, Ruth would risk trying anything. She'd already risked so much.

She popped open the bottle and shook a pill into her hand. She reached for the water glass on Ester's bedside table. Taking a deep breath, she lifted her sister's head, slid the pill into her mouth and forced her to drink.

Chapter Eight

Ester was alive. A long cry from her old self yet, but each day she grew stronger. Whether it was the pills from the doctor's bag or Momme's sworn regimen of good soup and rest, Ruth didn't know. And, she didn't care. Ester was better!

Ruth, however, was a bundle of nerves. She never did find out if the doctor was dead. There was no mention in the newspapers, although she kept checking. Time crawled on. She waited, jumping at any sound, imagining the clomping boots coming to the door for her.

One morning, Ruth came in from emptying the chamber pots to find Ester stirring a pot on the stove, humming to herself.

"What are you doing?" Ruth cried. "You shouldn't be on your feet."

Ester turned, spoon still in hand. "I wanted to surprise you with breakfast."

Ruth bustled over to take the spoon from Ester. "I appreciate the thought, but you're recuperating." She pulled out a chair and forced Ester into it.

Ester sighed and crossed her arms. "I'm recuperated, Ruth. It's been over a month."

"That's nothing for consumption. It can take years to recover."

Ester cracked a smile. "You're going to wait on me hand and foot for years?"

Ruth smoothed a hair back from Ester's face. "Why not? Anyway, for now, no early morning cooking sessions, *farshteyn?*"

Ester stuck her tongue out, but nodded.

Later, washing the dishes, she wondered how long they could carry on this way. It had been four years since Tatty and Abraham left. Four years! Yes, they were scraping by, but that was the accurate way to describe it. They were no more than surviving. Despite what she wrote in her letters to Abraham, there was no upside. She was not enjoying the challenges posed. She did not "feel blessed to discover a reserve of newfound strength," or whatever other positive phrasing she had used in her last letter. She was exhausted.

"I'm getting ready for work," she announced.

Ester and Momme both waved her off and continued their conversation. Ruth gritted her teeth as she left the room. It was not that she believed them ungrateful, but, wouldn't it be nice to stay comfortably at home this morning?

Well, she had no one to blame but herself for always trying to shield them from the realities outside their door—which couldn't be avoided in any case. She knew they had stress in their lives, too.

As she strode through the street a newspaper headline caught her eye:

Female Medical Supply Thief to be Caught and Prosecuted. Reward Offered!

Her stomach dropped. It had to be a coincidence. Someone must have robbed a hospital or something. Still, she rummaged in her pocket for a coin and paid the vendor.

Heart thumping, she unfolded the newspaper in the flapping wind and scanned the page.

It *was* about her.

The doctor was alive, at least. But the article was ridiculous. *Woman vigilante took down a grown man in his home! Deprives community of costly medical supplies. Justice must be served!* A crude sketch and description of her was included as well. Granted, it was shoddy artwork and a generic description, but enough to identify her, or at least attract suspicion. Jewish, dark hair, white skin, and green eyes. She thought of any number of desperate neighbors and girls at the factory. People might point fingers at any woman with dark hair and green eyes. How long until someone accused her? And what would happen to her when they did? Imprisonment? Hanging? Ruth's throat tightened at the thought.

She tore the paper in half and discarded it at soon as she could. Not that trashing one paper would make a difference. She hurried on to the factory. It was important to act as normal as possible.

THE DAY STRETCHED on in eternity. Despite her best efforts, her fingers fumbled and she made more mistakes than usual. As she tore out yet *another* stitch in frustration, she heard whispers to her right. She froze. Were the girls talking about her? She strained to make out what they were saying.

A blonde girl leaned in to her friends. "I heard she was

really a Jew and they picked up the whole family for the Pale of Settlement."

"I heard they hired a smuggler and got away to America!" the brunette sitting next to her said.

"A smuggler?" the blonde girl gasped. "Where'd they even find one?"

Indeed, Ruth thought. Where would they find one?

The brunette shrugged. "Who knows? Probably the shipyards like everything else on the Black Market these days."

They shushed and bent over their work as the foreman walked out from his office. Silence once again descended over the floor. But Ruth had heard enough.

A smuggler. She'd find a smuggler to get them out.

RUTH PEEKED over the bridge to the swirling activity on the ice below. Skaters zoomed by, chasing each other with laughter. Farther down the bank, the ice harvesters were hard at work, their movements precise and rhythmic. Ruth's heart clenched as she watched three children twirl together holding hands. She, Jeremiah and Abraham had once twirled like that. Was it really only a few years ago? It felt like a lifetime.

She shook her head hard to dispel the memories. She had to focus on the shipyard. She watched the behemoth metal tram power across the ice. It would have saved her time to take the tram, but she couldn't imagine the fare. It also seemed unnatural for delicate, fragile ice to carry something so heavy. With one last glance at the happy skaters, she turned and continued toward the *Vasilevskiy* side of the bridge with its towering red column.

As she exited the bridge, she felt her heart quicken in the bustle of the seaport. Huge wooden ships were mounted on platforms in varying stages of completion. Everywhere she looked, men were busy loading and unloading cargo. She realized only then she might not have thought this plan through. How exactly did she expect to locate a smuggler—walk up to some random sailor and ask if he was one? She almost chuckled at the sheer ridiculousness of the idea. Think, she scolded herself. What would Jeremiah do?

Be strategic, he would say. Consider how to locate the most information. What lowers a person's guard and gets them to talk?

Alcohol. Of course. And like most of the men in the city, the sailors probably conducted the majority of their business in the tavern. She scanned the nearby buildings for tavern signage. A shoe, a printing press and four swans with intertwined necks.

Four Swans. Perfect. She headed toward it.

Standing outside the tavern, Ruth adjusted her dress and took a deep breath. She'd never been in a tavern. Jeremiah and Abraham had, as soon as they were old enough to work at the factory. But she'd never been invited. It was not a place for respectable women, much less unmarried girls.

She looked over her shoulder as she gripped the door handle, almost in reflex, half expecting to see Tatty ready to grab her by the ear. She shook her head and opened the door, glad he couldn't see all the unseemly things she did on a daily basis now.

Chapter Nine

The tavern was dark and cloudy with tobacco smoke. It reeked of cabbage, vodka and the smell of men. These past years traversing the streets had made Ruth aware of the differences in unwashed male bodies verses female. There was a sharpness to a man's scent—a sort of predatory or even gamy pungency.

Ruth cringed. How foolish was she in coming here alone? But remembering how much danger she was already in, she straightened her shoulders and moved with purpose to the bar counter. If she acted like she was used to such places, perhaps real confidence and bravery would follow. She felt the men staring at her, sizing her up. She avoided their eyes, wondering how to start a conversation about smuggling. *Good day, could you point me to someone who can smuggle me out of the country...?*

The ridiculousness of her situation almost made her laugh. She bit her lip and tried to catch the eye of the barkeeper. The words would come.

The barkeeper wiped the counter with a greasy rag. He spoke in Russian. "I want no trouble, *shlyukha*."

Ruth swallowed. She hadn't been expecting a warm welcome, but had the man really called her a whore? She reflexively looked down at her dress and smoothed it. Wasn't she dressed respectfully enough? Her questioning panic was interrupted by the man's laughter.

"I take it back. You're more like a lost lamb in a den of wolves. Why are you here, sheep girl?"

She raised her chin. "I'm searching for someone with means to help me." She lowered her voice. "Someone with experience bypassing the checkpoints."

The man's smile faded. He crossed his arms. "And why do you feel I would know about that?"

Ruth breathed deep. "I don't know who would. I'm desperate."

The man picked up a glass and polished it. As he did, he leaned over the bar, so close she could smell onions on his breath. "We never had this conversation, do you understand? If I ever see you again, I have no memory of this."

Ruth nodded and began to push away from the bar. He touched her hand with the slightest of movement, and jutted his chin toward a man sitting by the window.

Relief flooded her, but before she could even thank him, he'd turned away.

Step one accomplished. But her battle was only beginning. She pulled her shawl tighter and moved hesitantly toward the man by the window.

He wore a faded green jacket and black fur hat like her father. But unlike Tatty, everything about the man–his posture, his expression–warned her to steer clear, stay away. He scowled into his glass of vodka. A bottle sat next to his elbow. A few men still regarded her hungrily, but the majority had returned to their *schmoozing*.

She pulled out the wooden chair across from the man

and perched on the seat. He took no notice and continued to stare into his glass. She waited a moment, then finally cleared her throat. His eyes rose to meet hers and a chill passed through her. This was a dangerous man. An eerie silence enclosed them as each waited for the other to speak. The echoes of laughter in the tavern suddenly seemed far away, like a different world.

Ruth summoned her false bravery again and her voice cracked as she spoke. "My family and I need to leave Russia."

She waited, the nakedness of her words hanging in the air.

The man's eyes traveled her over. She shifted her weight on her chair, wishing she could disappear.

Finally he spoke, his gruff voice barely a whisper. "It'll cost you."

Ruth nodded, mentally tallying the coins in the jar at home.

He poured himself another shot from the bottle. "There are multiple checkpoints along the way." He took a long sip from his glass. "You're a Jew, correct? Did you register?"

Ruth nodded, but her heart fell. She and Ester had registered and gotten their documents–they'd had to, to work in the factory–but it was a double-edged sword to be registered. You officially existed as a Jew. The government could turn on you at will. She'd heard of Jews, even with papers, turned away from checkpoints and forbidden to use their booked passage.

"My sister and I have papers," she said. "My mother does not. She never needed to register."

The man played with the glass in his hands. "Almost easier to start from scratch. No identity to replace." He poured more vodka and took another sip.

Ruth shifted again as she waited. She took in his work-worn hands darkened with dirt. His nails were cracked with black underneath. Everything about him made her skin crawl. Was it crazy to allow this scary man to have so much power over her future and safety? Momme and Ester's safety?

He finally spoke, so low she had to lean closer to hear. "Does it matter where you go?"

"America. We need to get to New York." Ruth licked her lips, her mouth suddenly dry. She longed for a drink from the bottle, though she never drank vodka. It was unladylike, according to Momme. Ha! If Momme could see her now.

The man snorted and laughed into his drink. "Why not aim for the moon?"

"My father and betrothed are already there and sending money for our passage."

"Then why come to me?" The man arched his eyebrows and frowned.

Again, Ruth's body prickled with fear. She should walk away. Wait for Tatty to send his final payment and book a safe passage. But the newspaper article was like a noose tightening around her neck. For about the millionth time since his passing, Ruth longed to seek advice from Jeremiah. He would know what to do. But she was on her own. The responsibility crushed heavy on her shoulders.

"I'm not sure it's safe to wait that long. My situation is—urgent."

A wolfish grin spread across the man's face. "Speed will cost extra."

She swallowed. "How much?"

"One hundred rubles."

Her stomach dropped. Was he serious? He might as well ask for her firstborn child.

"I don't have that kind of money," she said, struggling to sound calm.

"Not my problem." He reached for the bottle again. "Now, leave me alone and stop wasting my time."

Ruth stood, her legs trembling. Was that it? Her one chance for escape gone? She wrung her hands. "If I could somehow find the money?"

He shrugged. "You know where to find me."

She turned away, still shaking, and left the tavern for her long walk home. The price was impossible. Yet what if waiting was a death sentence? She'd never felt so afraid. Or so alone...

Chapter Ten

R uth sat cross-legged on the floor of Momme's room. She had two piles before her—one- of things that would generate barely any money at this point—basically worthless—- and the other—of potential contenders to sell.

The second pile was tiny. Too tiny to generate one hundred rubles, which was a greater sum than all their expenses for an entire year. Multiple years, even!

Her stomach twisted as she took in the remaining valuable items. They were Momme's silver candlesticks from Tatty and Momme's wedding, and Momme's mother's brooch. The biggest challenge of all might be persuading Momme to let her sell them in the first place. Ruth groaned at the thought.

"What are you doing in here?"

Ruth whirled around. Ester stood in the doorway with her hands on her hips.

"Why are you going through Momme's things?"

Ruth picked up the brooch and rubbed it with her skirt. "Uh, polishing and buffing?"

Ester scoffed. "Sure. Your bluffing is as bad as your buffing." She came to survey the items in the piles. "Aren't those Momme's 'Do not sell under any circumstances' items?"

She reached to pick the wedding ring from the pile, but Ruth stopped her by swatting her wrist. "I have no choice, Ester."

Ester's eyes widened. She looked again to the groupings on the floor. "Is this because I stopped working when I got sick? I can go back."

Ruth sighed. Naturally, Ester would blame herself. She wished she could explain the whole wretched situation, but how much could she share without endangering her sister?

"You are in no way responsible, Ester. And honestly, you returning to the factory would make no difference."

"To what? Are we being evicted?"

"Our home is safe. It's..." Ruth massaged her temples. "It's more complicated—"

Ester sat next to Ruth on the floor. "Are you in trouble?"

Ruth took in her sister's alarmed, but innocent gaze. She was massively botching this. Momme would be angry enough when Ruth suggested they sell her precious items. She sure wouldn't want Ester brought into it.

She patted Ester's hand. "You know what, Bird? How about you let me talk with Momme about it? You don't have to worry about anything." Ruth stood and brushed down her skirt. "It'll be okay."

Ester jumped to her feet. "I'm not a child anymore. Stop keeping me out!"

Ruth cringed. This was exactly what she feared–Ester growing up and pushing back. But why did it have to be now?

Perspiration gathered in her armpits. The neck of her

dress suddenly felt tight and stifling. "We need to leave Russia, Ester."

Ester shrugged. "Everyone's been saying that *forever*. But we can't make Tatty pay our fares faster."

Ruth lowered her gaze to her hands. "What if there was another way? A way we controlled our own departure?"

"What do you mean?"

Ruth fiddled with a string on her bodice. "A smuggler. I found a smuggler who can get us out."

Ester gasped. "You did what? Where?"

Ruth shrugged. "Where is not important."

"How much?" Ester whispered.

"One hundred rubles." Ruth's voice shook as she said it out loud.

She reached over and squeezed Ester's hand. "I know. It's a lot. But I'm figuring it out."

"But why now? Why a smuggler?"

Ruth chewed her lip as her mind spun, searching for an answer to give. Ester spoke before she could.

"I heard they're taking more Jews away. Like Riva. Are you afraid they'll come for us?"

Ruth offered a silent prayer of thanks. "Yes, Ester. That's it. Another girl from work disappeared two nights ago. I'm worried."

"We've made it this far. Sneaking off would be danger-ous, too, wouldn't it? So why act now in such haste?"

Ruth decided on another tactic. "We need to think of Momme. She has no papers. How can we guarantee we'll even get her through the checkpoints when Tatty's fares arrive?"

"Oy vey," Ester said. "I hadn't even thought—"

Ruth felt a twinge of guilt at all the details she was concealing from her sister. Like how the police might bang on the door at any moment and take her to possibly be hanged. The newspaper description and headline still haunted her—it flashed before her in the dark when she couldn't sleep. One nosy neighbor, and life as she knew it would be over.

"How will we convince her?" Ester asked.

"We'll broach it together at dinner."

Ruth tried to smile encouragingly. She prayed it wouldn't be a disaster.

ESTER WOULD NEVER SURVIVE a game of dice or a life of crime. Her clumsy nerves had her spilling the soup and twisting her mouth every time she looked in Ruth's direction. Momme gave them five minutes after prayers before asking, "Something on your minds, girls?"

Ester's eyes widened, and she seemed incapable of speaking. So much for sharing the burden. Ruth's mind spun, searching for an easy opener. Despite knowing this conversation needed to happen, she hadn't exactly figured out what to say.

"Well, uh..." Ruth stuttered. "We were thinking..."

Momme took a spoonful of her soup and waited patiently.

"Ruth wants us to use a smuggler to leave Russia," Ester burst out.

Ruth felt her pulse quicken. Not the opener she would have chosen!

Momme choked on her soup. "A smuggler? *Du farkirtst mir di yorn!*"

"Momme, she's doing it to protect you!" Ester interrupted. "To protect us."

"Is she?" Momme's eyes narrowed at Ruth.

Ruth swallowed against the sudden lump in her throat. "I feel it's necessary. Registration papers are harder to get... and more Jews are getting sent away."

Ester wrung her hands. "We're just sitting here, waiting. Any day could be our last!"

Momme stood and put her arms around Ester. "There, there, *sheifele*. We're in no more danger now than we've been the past four years."

Even as she comforted Ester, her eyes fixed coldly on Ruth. "How dare you fill her head with such nonsense! Tatty will send for us when he's ready. Until then we sit and wait like he said. He knows best."

Ruth jumped to her feet. "How will you cross the border when Tatty's tickets do arrive?"

Momme waved her off. "I'll get my papers filled like any other Russian citizen."

"And when they deny you, or take you away?"

Momme continued to stroke Ester's hair. "That won't happen."

Ruth leaned forward, her hands on the table. "Who do you know who's filed papers and been allowed to leave during the past year? Two years, even? Who has gotten approved?"

Momme blinked. "People have left—"

"Not to America they haven't. They've gone to family in the country. Or they've been taken to the Pale of Settlement. Or disappeared overnight like we would! The days of asking permission to sail to America are past."

"At least for Jews," Ester whimpered.

"Not just the Jews, Bird," Ruth said. "Anyone the czar wants to stop. But yes, the Jews have less chance than others."

"The czar wouldn't hold us hostage," Momme whispered.

Ruth leaned in to Momme. "I know you like to give the czar the benefit of the doubt, 'He wasn't there the day of the attack'... 'They weren't his orders.' I understand, I do. You want to still believe he has our best interests at heart since he is our leader. But, Momme, we need to act."

Ester nodded. "What if we keep waiting for Tatty, and they come for us, next? We'll never get to Tatty then!"

Momme moved toward her bedroom. "I need to think. Leave me be."

Ester and Ruth looked at each other. Ester started clearing the table. Ruth sank back into her chair and fiddled with her fork. She had known Momme would be difficult to convince—what with her faith in tradition and in men knowing best.

Ruth felt a surge of resentment at Tatty. How ridiculous that his word still meant law when he wasn't even here! How could he possibly know what was best when he hadn't lived in the country for four years? He had no idea how bad things had gotten. Until Tatty was cold in the ground, Momme would never think for herself.

Ruth brought the last of the dishes over to Ester and picked up the towel to dry the ones Ester had already washed. Neither spoke, each methodically going through the routine motions.

They were just finishing when Momme appeared.

"I'll go along with it," she whispered, laying a hand on Ruth's arm. "But, if this added rush puts us in harm's way, I don't know if I'll ever forgive you."

Ruth's stomach dropped. As if she *wanted* to take on the risk of a smuggler. Did Momme think she saw this as a flighty adventure? Her eyes tingled at the hot sting of tears. Before they spilled over, she gave Momme a curt nod.

"One more thing," Momme said. "You must find a way to pay without my mother's brooch."

Momme left the room again, and Ruth sagged against the wall, blinded by tears. Impossible. The brooch was their only hope...

Chapter Eleven

She barely slept that night, her mind tumbling and turning, analyzing every possibility and outcome. How could she raise the money for the smuggler without the brooch? Even if she could, would Momme ever forgive her if things went wrong? The thought was terrible, like a blanket suffocating her. Her own instincts had screamed danger when she met the smuggler—what if it was a trap? He'd take their life savings and turn them over to the czar's soldiers. Or worse, he'd sell them into slavery! But if they *didn't* hire the smuggler, what then?

A neighbor might turn her in for the reward and she'd soon be hanging from a noose. All night, Ruth's mind went to dark, dark places.

In the morning, she wished she could share her worries with Momme or Ester, but she knew it would only put them in further danger. She had to shoulder the burden alone. It was the only way she could ensure their safety, whether they realized it or not.

Days rolled by and the burden took more of a toll. Her

clothing fit looser and she was losing her hair. At work, girls called her out for making more mistakes.

"Pay better attention or we'll turn you in to the foreman for slowing us down!"

Ruth forged on and willed herself to hold it together. After work each day, she stopped by a pawn shop with an item and haggled like she never had before. The house became more and more bare as she stripped it down and sold things off. Lace curtains, tablecloths, even their menorah. Momme continued to protest against almost everything Ruth targeted.

"We've eaten every holiday meal on that tablecloth since you were born. My mother and I embroidered it for my wedding trunk!"

"We can't bring it all with us anyway. How will we carry all this to America? At least this way we can get some money for it."

Every discussion ended with Momme in tears and Ruth feeling even more guilty as she left with the item tucked under her coat.

One night, Ruth and Ester sat together, counting up the proceeds.

Ester scrunched her face in frustration. "We're still falling short."

Ruth pulled on her braid. "By a lot."

Ester looked around the room. "Is there anything left to sell?"

"Not enough to get what we need." Ruth sighed. "We need that brooch. It's our only hope."

Ester gathered coins back into the jar. "I don't think Momme will give in."

"I know." Ruth chewed her lip. "I'll think of something."

Ruth tossed and turned that night, thinking of the brooch. How else could she raise the money? She turned to her side and watched Ester's chest rise and fall steadily. She reached out one finger to stroke a lock of Ester's brown curly hair, which fanned out around her sister's angelic face on the pillow. Ester's face was finally starting to fill in again as she grew stronger and her cheeks were regaining their color. Despite all of the stress and worry, she didn't regret her actions to save Ester—not in the least. She'd steal the bag again tomorrow.

The bag! She could sell the medical supplies. They must be worth a lot, especially if the doctor was offering such a generous reward. Granted, that also increased the danger. She'd be revealing herself whenever she tried to sell them.

She closed her eyes and turned onto her back. It was a crazy idea. But it might be their only option if Momme wouldn't part with her brooch.

The next morning looked like snow. As she walked to work, Ruth leaned into the bone-cutting breeze, pulling her threadbare coat tighter. There were more soldiers than usual patrolling the streets. Maybe there was more unrest with the rebel groups? She hadn't been paying attention to political news lately. She hoped there weren't more strikes or shutdowns brewing. As if escape weren't difficult enough...

She arrived at the factory to find a cluster of girls outside with their heads together. What was going on this morning?

She was about to join them when a hand clamped down on her arm. She looked up to see Oriana, the brunette girl who sat a few seats away from her in the factory. She was the one who'd been speaking about the smuggler. They'd spoken a few times since, but nothing much. Oriana gestured to Ruth to follow her into a side alley between buildings.

"You need to go. You can't be here," Oriana said.

"What?" Ruth pulled her coat even tighter. "What are you talking about?"

Oriana shifted from foot to foot and peeked out to the street. "There's been another medical supply theft. They're calling her *Ognyena*. The thief who can fell male doctors to the ground."

Despite the danger of this situation, Ruth felt a flash of pride. But wait, she had nothing to do with the second incident. Had she inspired someone else to take a chance—another desperate woman, perhaps?

Oriana's voice dropped as if afraid someone was eavesdropping. "The doctors are banding together to double the reward. Soldiers, police–everyone's patrolling."

Ruth's stomach roiled. The soldiers had been patrolling for *her*. There was no way she'd be able to sell off the medical supplies now. Oriana was studying Ruth, waiting for her reaction.

Ruth tried to keep her voice steady. "Why are you telling me this? What does it have to do with me?"

Oriana raised her eyebrows. "Really? The sketch has been all over the papers for weeks. It looks just like you! Why do you think I mentioned the smuggler?"

"You did that on purpose? Why not turn me in?"

Oriana shrugged. "I'm not a snitch. With your sister sick, you had your reasons. But I can't be the only one who's figured it out. With the reward doubled, it's only a matter of time before someone overcomes their scruples."

Ruth knew she needed to run. But her feet suddenly felt leaden. She struggled to breathe, like her throat was closing. What if she returned home and soldiers were waiting? What if they stopped her in the street?

Oriana reached and took Ruth's hand. "Go home, Ruth. Whatever you need to do to get the smuggler arranged, do it. Leave the city as soon as possible."

Oriana turned away and left, as if any further association with Ruth would taint her. Ach, how was this Ruth's life now?

She lowered her headscarf and tried to pull her coat collar up to cover her face. She needed to keep her head and think of next moves. Oriana was right. They needed to leave, immediately.

She darted out of the alley and stayed as close to the buildings as she could for cover. Weaving between people with her eyes on the ground, avoiding eye contact. She wished she could become invisible. That no one would notice her, recognize her from the drawing.

She was five minutes from home when a deep voice called out.

"You, there!"

Ruth froze. Was he referring to her or someone else? She looked around, hoping he meant someone else.

"You, in the red scarf!"

He meant her. Spots clouded her vision and she feared she'd pass out. Should she run, or would that lead them straight to Momme and Ester? She turned slowly, praying whatever was about to transpire would be quick and not too painful.

The soldier stalked over. He looked her up and down. A hot flush crept up her neck as she waited for him to speak.

"You dropped this."

"What?" Her brain felt unable to process his words.

He handed her an embroidered handkerchief with Momme's signature flower in the corner. "Your handkerchief. You dropped it back there."

Her knees wobbled as she accepted the handkerchief. He stood waiting. She finally mustered a smile and nod of thanks. Could he hear her pounding heart? She felt like he must, the way it hammered in her chest.

He walked away. As soon as he turned the corner, she broke into a run. She raced home as fast as her legs could carry her.

Luckily, neither Momme nor Ester were there. They must be at the market. That made it easy. She didn't even hesitate—she went straight to Momme's room and opened the bottom drawer. Her hands shook as she removed the brooch from its bag. There was no other choice now. She prayed Momme would one day forgive her.

Chapter Twelve

The shop owner raised his eyebrows. "It's a beautiful brooch. Are you sure you want to part with it?"

Ruth stared at her feet. "Can't eat a brooch, right?"

The man shook his head and handed her the cash. "What desperate times we've come to."

Ruth thanked him and tucked the cash into the front of her blouse. She almost expected him to stop her. Scold her for her deception. He hadn't even questioned her on the brooch's origins, which made her feel even more guilty. She wondered if she'd ever be worthy of trust again. If Momme would ever trust her again.

She hurried back out to the street and hewed close to the buildings as she walked. The money felt like it was burning in her blouse.

Rain drops began to spit down on her head as she made her way to the bridge. Gone were the skaters this time. Instead, the ice below was desolate. Although the shipyard was as bustling and busy as ever, Ruth felt an almost forbidding heaviness in the air as she crossed the bridge. She bristled as a man passed by her and quickened her pace. The red column bristling with ship fronts towered ominously over her as she stepped off the bridge.

For the first time, the danger of what she was setting into motion truly hit her. Shivering, she leaned against the nearest wall for support, rain drops trickling down her nose. Once she surrendered this money to the smuggler, there was no turning back. She literally held their life savings—the only money they had left—tucked away in her blouse. Once it was gone, they were destitute and reliant on this smuggler with his wolfish grin.

What if he took her money and instead of securing their papers he went straight to the police or soldiers? For the thousandth time she wished Jeremiah was here. Not that he'd have all the answers, but he'd share the burden of the decision.

"Help me, *bruder*," she whispered.

She took a deep breath. What would Jeremiah do? The answer came to her, like a reassuring squeeze on her shoulder. He would act. He was never afraid to do what he had resolved to do. She could almost hear his voice whispering in her ear.

"*You gotta have faith, shvester. Faith in God and faith in yourself.*"

Faith. A big ask in her current predicament. But at the same time, what choice did she have? As Oriana had pointed out, any moment someone could be turning her in for the reward money. And who would blame them? These were desperate times and people needed food on the table. She believed this was their best chance for escape, and she had to trust her instincts.

Ruth forced herself to approach the Four Swans

Tavern. Pulling herself to her full height to project confidence, she opened the tavern door and stepped inside.

It was dark. She had forgotten how poorly lit the tavern was. Her heart hammered as she waited for her eyes to adjust. A group of men blocked her view of the table where the smuggler had sat. Would he be there again? What if he'd taken a job helping someone else escape, and wouldn't be back for weeks, or forever?

The room was busier than last time. The rain must have forced people inside. She smelled wet wool, cabbage and onions. The barkeeper avoided her gaze, and she hoped she wouldn't need him for anything. As she threaded through the tables, the gaze of men calculated her appearance. The wad of cash still burned against her skin. How vulnerable it made her—a woman alone with money in a rough part of the city.

She glimpsed the smuggler slumped over a vodka bottle. Her heart leapt. He was here! She hurried over to the table and slid into the chair opposite him.

"Hello again," Ruth said.

The smuggler grunted and poured another drink.

She waited for him to say more. When he didn't, she asked, "Do you remember me?" She heard her voice waver like a child's.

He gave a small nod, but still did not speak.

"I have what you requested. How soon could we leave?"

The man reached across the table with an open hand.

"Not until you give me more details." Ruth set her jaw and tried to appear confident, although her stomach was churning. This man was more infuriating than ever!

He pulled his hand back slowly took another sip of vodka. His scrutinizing gaze swept over her. Measuring, deciding. She'd never felt more laid open and wanting.

Finally, he spoke, his voice gravelly as if with disuse. "You're in a rush, right? Three of you, all women?"

Ruth nodded. "And we need papers."

His face split into that wolfish grin. "Not necessarily."

Ruth shivered, despite the warmth of the room. She tugged her shawl tighter. "How can we get past the check-points without papers?"

He ignored her. He sipped the dregs of his vodka and poured himself another. Some vodka splashed over the glass and onto the table

Should she get up and leave? Insist upon papers or else? Ruth shifted uncomfortably on her chair.

"You realize this will be a dangerous experience, *devochka?*" His eyes narrowed, his expression suddenly grave. "And it's permanent. You can never return."

Ruth sat straighter in her chair. "We have nothing to return to. Everything we need is in America. We just need to get there."

The man studied her, judging her answer. "We'll leave tomorrow at nightfall. Prepare yourself for an arduous jour-ney." He stretched out his hand again.

Ruth reached into her blouse and retrieved the wad of cash. But still, she hesitated. "How will we go?"

"I can't tell you. The less you know the better. You'll have to trust me."

There it was again. That leap of faith and trust. She didn't trust him. But could she? With her life? She studied him more closely, his shabby jacket and hat, his shaking hand as he poured another glass of vodka. His face in rest, however, was potentially a different story. She saw the cloud of sadness in his eyes. But there were laugh lines, too. Certainty settled into her stomach. Like hers, the man's life hadn't always been this way. She once again felt Jeremiah's presence reminding her to have faith.

She gave him the wad of cash and he took it without a word.

"Can you at least tell me where we'll meet you?" she asked.

The man laughed and shoved the money into his pocket. He pulled out a stub of pencil, scrawled down an address on a napkin, and pushed it toward her. He then waved her off, dismissing her again.

Ruth rose from the table, her face hot. Ugh, men and their entitled attitudes. She folded the napkin and tucked it into her blouse where the cash had been, and stalked from the tavern. She was halfway across the bridge toward home when it hit her—she didn't even know the man's name.

"WHAT DID YOU DO?" Momme screamed. "Do you have any idea how important that brooch was?"

Ruth wrung her hands. "We needed the money, Momme. We need to leave now."

Momme's eyes narrowed. "What is really going on? Why are you so desperate for us to leave?"

Ruth looked to the floor.

"What's really going on, *sheifele?*" Momme asked. "And don't give me that story about papers and fear again. Because I know that's not enough to make my girl steal from me."

Ruth felt the searing burn of tears behind her eyes. She tried to blink them back, but every emotion she'd been tamping down came crashing to the surface. She collapsed in Momme's arms and began to sob. She needed her mother.

Momme steered her to the bed. They sat down together and Momme stroked Ruth's hair and held her close. "Tell me everything."

Ruth hiccupped and took a deep breath. "Remember when Ester was sick? It wasn't just your magical soup that made her better."

Momme's brows furrowed. "I don't understand. What else could it have been? The doctor wouldn't come."

Ruth played with the fringe on the blanket beneath her. "True, he would not. But more happened at his house than I told you."

Momme's hand tightened on Ruth's. "Did he force himself on you? Are you with child? Is that why you're in such a hurry to leave?"

Ruth shook her head. "No—no, he tried to, but I wouldn't let him. I fought back, Momme. I fought back hard. Almost— too hard."

Momme pressed her lips into a straight line.

"I thought I'd killed him." Ruth's throat tightened, until she could barely choke out the words. "He fell back. There was blood. I took the medicine bag. I ran away..."

Momme gasped. "You're the thief in the newspaper! The one they're searching for?"

Ruth's body shook.

Momme gathered her into another hug and rocked her. "Oh, why didn't you tell me?"

"If you didn't know, you could deny."

Momme pulled back and looked at Ruth. "You protecting me. It should be the other way around. I'm the mother." She smoothed a damp tendril of hair from Ruth's face.

"*Oy vey*, we have a lot to do to get ready. We leave tomorrow, you said?"

Ruth nodded. "At nightfall."

Ester appeared at the door, waving an envelope. "It's from Tatty. He paid our tickets!"

Ruth froze. "What do we do?"

Momme grabbed for the envelope from Ester. "Let me see." She pulled out the letter and scanned it. She looked back to Ruth. "You say this man has a plan?"

Ruth nodded.

Momme chewed her lip. "I'd still have to apply for papers. What if—like you said—they don't allow me to leave? Or send me far away? And we couldn't book passage till next week at the earliest..."

Ruth waited. Would Momme change her mind? Should they try to use the tickets?

Momme shook her head. "It's too risky. We'll stick with the plan."

"But what will we tell Tatty?" Ester asked.

Momme hesitated. Then she crumpled the letter in her hand. "Nothing. We never got this letter. We left before it got here, *fershtay?*"

Ester opened her mouth to say something and then shut it and nodded solemnly.

Momme locked eyes with Ruth. "Everything that happened these past four years, stays between us. The men need never know how bad and dangerous things got. We'll tell them we got jobs and paid our own passage because we missed them so much."

Ester glanced between Ruth and Momme. Ruth could tell she wanted to ask about what had transpired between them. But she just nodded.

Momme motioned to the door. "Now, go, get packing! We've got work to do."

Ester scurried out the door leaving Ruth alone with Momme again.

"Thank you," Ruth said.

"Remember, *sheifele,* you don't need to carry the burden alone."

Chapter Thirteen

R uth scanned the house. The walls were empty. Every valuable item had been sold or packed. They'd leave behind the furniture and everything else they could not carry.

Momme and Ester were still cleaning in the back of the house. Momme insisted on every thing being scrubbed down and left in a state of perfection. No amount of reasoning could change her mind.

Ruth pulled out a chair and sat, putting her elbows on the kitchen table. She looked at its worn, wooden surface. She knew every nick and scratch, every condensation ring.

This was the last day she'd ever sit here. She hoped another family would love it as much as they had. This table where she'd eaten every family meal. Where she'd played cards with Jeremiah and Abraham. Where she'd learned to read the Bible with Tatty.

Tears prickled her eyes. She'd never see any of this again. They could never return to Russia.

But she was fine with leaving. Wasn't she? That's what she'd told Momme. Why should they mourn a place that had treated them so horribly? Still, she'd had a good childhood here. Friends, relatives, neighbors. It was the only home she'd ever known.

She wiped her eyes and looked at the clock. A few hours until sundown, until their lives changed forever.

She noticed the white envelope from Tatty sticking out of Momme's last-minute packing pile on the edge of the table. In addition to the tickets, he'd included bank drafts. She knew Momme meant to stitch the cash in their clothing. Ruth picked up the envelope to begin sewing, but then hesitated. She couldn't help remembering the hurt in Momme's eyes, when Ruth had confessed to selling the brooch. Could Ruth make it up to her? She tucked the drafts in her blouse and grabbed her shawl.

"I'm running out for one last errand," she called.

She hurried from the house before Momme could stop her. She was being foolish, tempting fate by going out in broad daylight one last time. She didn't need Momme to tell her. But she felt compelled to try and buy back the brooch before they left for good.

THE BELL to the pawn shop rang as she ducked through the door. Although no one else was there besides the owner, she kept her shawl up over her head until she reached the counter.

"The emerald brooch." Her eyes scanned the room, trying to find it in the display cases. "I was in here yesterday..."

The owner shrugged. "It's gone."

"Gone?" Her voice rose an octave. "How? Who is shopping for a brooch during these times?"

The owner wet his lips and turned away. "I can't remember exactly– but it's not here. I'm sorry, *baryshnya*."

He was lying. She leaned in over the case. "What did you do with my brooch? Sell it on the black market?"

"It was no longer yours. You sold it to me." The owner's mouth tightened. "Now leave my store before I call for the *Politsiya*."

Ruth slammed her hands on the counter, but when he squared his shoulders, she took a step backwards. She met his eyes as she tightened her shawl. "You're scum, profiting off people's belongings this way."

The man shrugged. "I'm surviving." He gestured to the door.

Ruth pushed it open, the bell taunting her as she left.

MOMME STOOD with her hands on her hips waiting by the door. "Where have you been? We were worried."

Ruth took in the worry lines around Momme's eyes. Her genuine expression of fear. Every bit of resolve and hardness Ruth had built inside herself dissolved and crumbled. "I—I—"

Momme's arms encircled her. "What happened? Did soldiers bother you?"

Ruth shook her head. "I tried—"

Momme rubbed circles on Ruth's back, like when she was a little girl. But it made Ruth feel even more guilty.

"I tried to get your brooch back," she managed to say, hiccupping. "It was gone."

Momme's back circles continued and she added gentle shooshing noises. "It wasn't meant to be. I've made my peace with it."

Ruth wiped tears away and saw Ester hovering nearby with a glass of water. Ruth took it.

"Thank you." She took a sip of water."I suppose I needed one last good cry."

Momme laughed. "I had mine last night."

Ester looked back and forth between them. "Are you having doubts?"

"No, *sheifele.*" Momme patted Ester on the arm. "Just letting go."

Ruth nodded. "Now, we have some sewing to do. We need to hide those drafts in our clothes."

Momme pulled out her sewing kit and rubbed her hand lovingly over the top before opening it. It was too big to carry, and Ruth knew it must be crushing Momme to leave it behind.

Momme expertly prepared needle and thread for each of the girls, like she did when they were children, and they sat in their usual chairs for one last sewing circle.

At last, the sun drooped in the sky and shadows crept between buildings. Momme stood by the window watching the lamplighters. She dropped the curtain and turned to Ruth and Ester. "It's time."

They pulled up their shawls and took their knotted blanket bundles containing their few precious items and all the food they could gather. They moved stiffly as they adjusted to wearing every item of clothing they owned. Ruth took one last look around the house. She noticed a last sunbeam illuminating the dust in the air. Their footsteps echoed in the empty room as they moved to the door. It closed behind them with one final click.

They remained silent as they skittered through the cold, dark streets, their breath frosting in the air. They clung to the shadows, away from prying eyes. As they neared the meeting spot, Ruth peeked around a corner, dismayed to see two soldiers come into view. She turned back and attempted to wave off Momme and Ester, but it was too late.

"What have we here?" one soldier asked. He was tall and lanky, looming over his partner.

"Some ladies out after curfew." The shorter soldier grinned and rubbed his hands together. "Looking for a good time, perhaps?"

Cold crept up Ruth's neck. What now? How could they escape this?

The short soldier stepped closer. Ruth felt Ester clutch her arm.

Momme moaned behind them. Startled, the soldiers craned their heads to examine the dark shadows.

"Who goes there? Is something amiss?" the tall soldier called.

Momme stepped into the light with a huge round belly and her hand at her back.

"Oh, the pain!" She stopped to lean against the wall and breathed heavily.

Ruth, catching on, turned back to the soldiers. "Can't you see it's her time? Move away, we're trying to get her to my aunt's house for help!"

The short soldier looked to the other with a panicked expression.

The tall soldier's eyes narrowed. "Why do you have your bags packed? Where is your aunt's house?"

Ruth gestured ahead. "Only a few more blocks."

"We need supplies for the delivery," Ester said. "Rags for the bleeding and such."

The tall soldier looked to the short one. "Should we escort them?"

The short one shrugged.

"Oh, let us go," Momme hissed from the wall. "Keep your nattering—the baby will be born in this alley."

The short soldier gestured them on. The tall one made as if to follow, but Ruth put her arm around Momme and hurried them at such a pace, he gave up and turned back.

Once a few blocks of distance were behind them, Ruth let out the breath she'd been holding.

"Momme, you were incredible!"

Momme released a strangled laugh. "At least these bundles are good for something!"

Ruth put her hands through Ester and Momme's arms. "We have a long way to go yet, before we're out of danger."

Momme patted her rounded stomach. "I'll keep my bundle here, just in case."

Ruth squeezed Ester and Momme's arms. "At least we're in it together."

Ester pulled Ruth in closer and smiled.

Chapter Fourteen

The smuggler leaned against a wall, smoking a cigarette. "I was about to give up."

"We hit an unexpected checkpoint." Ruth told him.

The smuggler's posture changed, his shoulders tensing. "You weren't followed, were you?"

"No. We got creative."

He nodded slightly as he looked the three of them over. He stubbed out the cigarette on the wall and turned away. "Let's get moving."

"Shouldn't you at least tell us where we're going? Your name? Anything?" Ruth asked.

The smuggler shrugged. "The less we know about each other, the better."

Ruth looked to her mother and sister. Momme nodded and gestured for them to follow. Ester patted Ruth's arm and they began their journey.

～

HE MOVED AT A BRISK PACE. They almost had to run to keep up. After what felt like hours, blisters began to form on the back of Ruth's heels, and she worried about Momme, whose face was pinched from exertion. The road became more desolate, buildings spaced farther apart. The piles of snow grew larger, and the cold more bitter. Ruth's nose felt like an icicle and she'd lost feeling in her hands.

Ruth had never been this far outside the city. The silence seemed deafening, the only sound their feet crunching softly on the snow. In St. Petersburg, even at night, you could hear some action in the streets. Despite the curfew, there were always drunkards returning from the taverns or carts clomping past to prepare for morning market. Sometimes you could even hear the rhythmic marching of nighttime soldiers on their rounds.

The men—her father, Abraham, and his father—must have experienced this eerie quiet, when *they* had fled. For the first time, she appreciated what they went through. They had been forced to leave suddenly with no money or destination. And they'd had no smuggler.

She looked to the smuggler for any hint to his plan. Would they walk till morning or would they meet a wagon or some form of transport? She remembered seeing maps of Russia in school and being impressed by its vast breadth. But, now, instead of feeling awe, she just imagined how far they had to go and how far the czar's power reached.

Ruth glanced at the sky—it was lightening to a shade of purple. Dawn was approaching. The smuggler changed his direction, leading them away from the road. Ester grabbed Ruth's arm as their feet sank into deep snow. She tripped, going down to one knee. Her bundle dropped before her.

"Are you all right?" Ruth asked, helping her sister regain her footing.

"I'm going to collapse."

Momme stooped to check if anything had fallen from the wrapped blanket, then handed it back to Ester. "Ruth, will you ask if we'll be stopping soon? We need a break."

Ruth looked ahead. Did the smuggler even know they'd stopped?

She spotted his fading figure about one hundred paces ahead. He'd soon vanish into a band of trees. Did she dare call out?

She cupped her hands to her mouth. "Caw, Caw!"

Momme's head jerked. "Are you mad?"

"How else do you expect me to get his attention?" Ruth hissed.

"Caw, Caw!" She called again.

The figure stopped and turned.

"Come!" Ruth grabbed Momme and Ester's arms and pulled them, staggering to where he stood. A sharp pain stabbed Ruth's side, making it hard to breathe. She prayed he wouldn't stride off immediately again.

In the dim light she could see his lips twitch as they drew near.

"Curious birds out today."

Ruth frowned. "Maybe if you looked over your shoulder occasionally?"

He gave a small nod. "We'll stop for rest now."

Ester and Momme exhaled in relief.

"Where?" Ruth asked.

The smuggler pointed to a plume of smoke coming from behind the trees. "There's a farm."

He began to walk again. Ruth's mind flooded with questions. Did he know the farmer? Was the farmer trustworthy? Why did he have to be so cryptic? It was one thing to be a man of few words, but couldn't he at least make those words reassuring or fully informative?

They trudged to the farm, where the smuggler pointed to a barn. "Make yourselves comfortable. I'll be along shortly."

Ester reached the barn door first, and hesitantly pulled it open. A cow mooed and hoofbeats scuffled.

"There are animals," she said, her voice trembling.

"We are on a farm, Bird." Ruth pushed the door fully open. She tried to act confident in front of Ester, but her own heart was thumping. She had never been in a barn. Aside from a few emaciated donkeys and carthorses, they had not seen animals in years. The products of animals—yes. But, even that had been awhile.

They tiptoed into the barn. Ruth gagged at the smell of manure. The barn had seen better days. The rafters had cobwebs and a few empty birds' nests. There was a bucket in the corner to catch drips from the roof. Most of the stalls were empty, but there was one scrawny cow and two small horses. Momme pointed to a rickety ladder leading to a hayloft.

"Should we go up there?"

Ester wrinkled her nose. "I don't trust that ladder."

They sat on the cold floor until the smuggler came with a plate of bread and a pitcher. He handed the plate to Ruth and entered the stall with the cow. She heard a rough, squelching sound, and peered in to see him tugging on the cow's teats.

After a few minutes, he came out and offered the full pitcher to Ruth. "There's a privy out back you can use. Rest, we have a hard night ahead."

He left the women alone in the barn. Ruth took a sip from the pitcher and passed it to her mother. The three eagerly drank the creamy milk and split the crumbly bread. After using the privy, they sank into the straw and fell fast asleep.

❧

RUTH WOKE, startled by a hand on her arm.

In the gray evening light, the smuggler's face looked more weathered than usual. His eyes had bags beneath them. "It's time," he said.

She woke Momme and Ester and they gathered their things. The smuggler waited for them outside. He took a long slug from his flask. He gestured, offering it to the women.

There was an awkward pause, and Momme shook her head. He shrugged and began to walk, and the women followed.

The cow's moo echoed as they cut across the snowy field to the road. Where was the smuggler taking them now? Ruth suddenly missed the barn, where she had had felt safe and almost warm. She silently cursed the rising fear in her chest.

They trudged on. She watched the smuggler's back, his boots clomping on the road. On either side, the gray woods seemed to stretch forever. Her feet slipped on the muddy slush with every step, until she felt lightheaded with frustration. She had never felt so out-of-control, so completely out of her element. She'd always taken comfort in *deciding* things, but there was nothing for her to decide here. Whether she ate, slept, or froze to death—it was all in the hands of that man, that near stranger, that dark figure that went *clomp, clomp, clomp* so endlessly and hatefully.

The sun finally rose to pierce the nighttime sky. This

time, however, instead of stopping to sleep in a warm barn, they only had a small enclave with trees for shelter. The smuggler scrounged up some berries and they ate the last of the food from their bundles. They then slept in shifts to protect against discovery.

It was the same for the next two days. Ruth had no idea where on that vast expanse of the map they were, at this point. Were they close to the border? How much further must they travel? Was there even water at the edge of Russia? Where must they go to catch a boat to America? She hated herself for how little she knew.

She woke on the fourth evening to the smell of cigarette smoke. She sat up to find the smuggler peering down at her.

"We finish the walking portion of the voyage today."

"Are we out of Russia then?" Ruth asked.

The smuggler shook his head. "Almost. The train will take us out." He tossed his cigarette to the ground. "Say nothing, and let me do the talking."

She stumbled to her feet. As usual when she woke, her muscles screamed with pain. But a train! She trembled with desperate yearning—to sit on a train and travel without this endless trudging.

THE TRAIN WAS NOT FAR from their sleeping spot. It sat alone on the track in a desolate field—an odd place to stop, with no station or town nearby. The smuggler ran ahead and knocked on the door of a freight car.

It slid open. She saw the flash of a lantern—the smuggler seemed to be handing over a package.

Money. This was planned, Ruth realized. The train had been waiting for them. How long had it stood there? The smuggler grew ever more complex with his far-reaching contacts and pre-arranged logistics. How often had he done this?

The man with the lantern jumped down and disappeared into the night, and the smuggler gestured for the women to climb aboard. He lit a match to show them a few wooden crates and an empty bucket in the corner. Ruth shivered—it was no warmer inside the car than outside—and wrinkled her nose at the dank, moldy smell.

After the match went out, the smuggler slid the door closed, shutting out the moonlight. Now they were in total darkness. Ruth dropped her bundle. She located one of the crates by feel, and sat down. After a few moments she heard a clattering sound. She realized it was the smuggler urinating in the metal bucket. Would the indignity never end?

She knew she'd have to make use of the bucket, too, before long, but she wanted to put it off as long as possible.

She heard Ester's stomach growling and closed her eyes. Her own stomach ached and roiled. Aside from a few more snatched berries, they had barely eaten since the farm. Her mouth salivated at the mere memory of warm milk and bread. How many days ago had that been?

The smuggler's voice came out of the darkness. "Everybody all right?"

"Yes," Momme answered quietly.

Ruth felt some tree bark shoved into her hand. "Here," he said. "It's bark. It tastes awful, but it relieves the hunger pangs."

Ruth gnawed on the bark. "Why do you do this?"

"Do what?"

"It can't just be about the money."

He chuckled. "Believe what you must." She heard him drink from his flask. "Get some rest."

⁓

RUTH WOKE WITH AN UNEASY FEELING. It was still pitch black. She could hear Momme's light snores and feel Ester's warm body next to her. The steady movement of train on the tracks rumbled beneath her. Then why did she feel so unsettled?

There was a rustling by her skirts and she felt a light touch on her leg. She sat straight up. "Who's there?"

She heard someone's light breaths, then a scraping sound.

A match sprang to light. The smuggler loomed, the black eye of his gun pointed straight at her. No, not at her— at the man who huddled by her feet, his fingers still clutching one of the bank drafts sewn into her dress. It was the man who had let them on the train.

"Drop it!" the smuggler said.

The man jumped to his feet with his hands raised. Ruth felt Momme and Ester stir next to her. They were also awake and watching.

"Next time I'll shoot first."

"Don't make an enemy of me," the man said. "I'm warning you."

The smuggler cocked his gun with a click. "I'll take my chances."

The smuggler's match flickered and went out and they were plunged back into complete darkness. Ruth's heart pounded in her chest as she waited for the man's next move. She wrapped her arms tight around her knees as if that would protect her.

Finally, she heard the shuffle of feet and the clatter of the door. There was a blast of cold air and the rushing sound of wind. The man had departed the car.

Ester's hand found hers. "Are you all right?"

"Yes, I'm fine," Ruth said. Her voice somehow sounded steadier than she felt. Her heart still pounded in her chest. How had the man gotten into the car with them? She didn't know. He must have planned this all along—ridden on the train and changed cars when the train stopped or slowed down. She'd been completely oblivious, sleeping the deep sleep of exhaustion.

Ruth heard the smuggler tug the door closed again. The women huddled even closer together as they lay back down. But it wasn't until she felt the smuggler settle himself on the floor by her head–that Ruth's heart finally slowed. She forced herself to lie still as her mother and sister's breathing steadied. The smuggler lit a cigarette. For the first time, Ruth found the smell of tobacco comforting. Her eyelids drooped and she drifted back to sleep.

Chapter Fifteen

The train ride felt like eternity. It was dark in the car even in daytime, except for streaks of light through the cracks in the walls. Aside from that, Ruth would have no idea if it was day or night. She also had no idea how many days they'd even been on the train. Two? Three? It all blended, as had their entire journey. Sometimes the train slowed down or stopped for checkpoints or for refueling. No one entered the car or bothered them again, but Ruth had trouble relaxing after the events with the intruder. She kept jolting awake, her heart pounding. The smuggler never left their side, but still Ruth feared someone evil creeping toward her silently in the darkness.

Her stomach continued to growl—tree bark only did so much. It would have been far worse without water, which the smuggler now produced from his bag and passed out in tiny rations. Despite it, Ruth felt thirstier with every hour.

Momme tried to pass the time with her storytelling, but this too grew tiresome as the hours stretched on. The smuggler, though, surprised them with some poetry recitation. His voice had a rich timbre, warm and melodic. Ruth found herself marveling again at the strangeness. Who was this man? How could he be so comfortable both aiming a gun and reciting poetry in the dark?

A screech pierced the air and the train threw them backwards as it slid to a stop. Ruth's ears rang in the silence. Was this a checkpoint? Were they at their destination?

A series of knocks sounded on the outside of the car. Ruth heard the smuggler get to his feet, and a click as he undid the latch on the door and slid it open. A blaze of dazzling light blinded her. She squinched her eyes shut, unable to bear it. Finally, she opened her eyes again, squinting and blinking. She looked to Momme and Ester, but even their faces appeared strange and unfamiliar after relying on her other senses for so long.

The smuggler's voice startled her. "Welcome to Germany, ladies."

"Really?" Ester gasped. "We made it?"

Momme wiped tears from her eyes.

Ruth knew she should move, get up, start gathering their things. But for some reason she felt bewildered, frozen to this spot where she had sat for so long. Like her bones were suddenly forged with metal and too heavy to move.

The smuggler crouched down next to her. He put a hand on her shoulder. "You're finally safe. It's over."

Safe. Did she even know what that word meant anymore? Would she know how to function when she wasn't in a constant state of fear?

She saw the kindness in his eyes. He nodded and squeezed her shoulder. He seemed to know all the questions and thoughts running through her mind.

"You're strong. You made it" He pulled her to her feet.

Climbing down from the train car, Ruth almost fell. Her muscles ached and her head swam from lack of food and water. She turned to help Momme and Ester clamber down.

"I'm so sore," Ester complained. "How far is it?"

"Not far, *sheifale*. We're almost there," Momme said.

Ruth smiled. She had no idea if that was true, but she loved her mother for saying it.

It was early morning. Ruth could tell by the gray light, the freshness in the air. There was also that peaceful quiet when few humans are up and about. They were in a train yard. A few men unloaded cars from the front of the train.

Were they close to a boat that could bring them to America? She knew nothing about Germany, other than that it was a new country, free from Russia's rule. Ruth sniffed the air, hoping to smell the sea. All she could smell was the stirrings of spring.

The smuggler was a few yards away, smoking as usual.

"Where are we?" Ruth asked him.

"Germany," he said.

"I got that part. Where in Germany? Where's the boat? What's the plan?"

"I told you, no plans."

"But we're not in Russia anymore," Momme said. "Surely, you can share the plan with us now."

He rubbed his chin and thought for a moment. "Hamburg. We're going to Hamburg. You'll catch a boat from there to America tomorrow."

Ester grabbed Ruth's arm. Ruth clapped her own hand on top of Ester's. If she had more strength she'd literally jump for joy. They were leaving for America tomorrow!

The smuggler stubbed out his cigarette. "Come, let's get food and a place to stay."

He led them away from the train yard. They passed by a few small houses, but the smuggler didn't stop. They continued walking until the sky was fully crisp and blue with fluffy clouds overhead. Finally, they reached a town, bustling with energy and people opening their shops.

The smuggler moved with confidence, leading the way with purpose. Clearly, he'd been here before. A sign with a painting of a bed for an inn came into view. Below it, a woman swept the front steps. She looked up as they approached, her face lighting into a smile.

"Gerta!" The smuggler greeted the woman in Russian. "I have brought you special guests."

Gerta stopped sweeping. "Welcome to Germany, ladies. Let's get you some food and a hot bath."

Gerta bustled them into the inn and seated them at a worn wooden table. Within minutes, she reappeared with bread, sausages and large glasses of something golden. Ruth could hardly bear the smell of the bread. It overpowered her. She tore at it like an animal, sank her teeth into it in heavenly bliss. She almost fainted from pure delight.

Ruth looked up and met the eyes of the smuggler. She almost started laughing—she must look ridiculous with her mouth so full. His own eyes crinkled a little. She gained control of herself and offered him a piece, which he accepted with a nod.

Ruth picked up the glass with the strange golden beverage and sniffed at it curiously. Bubbles rose to the top. She took a sip and a grainy, almost sweetish taste filled her mouth. She'd never tasted anything like it before. She took another sip, trying to decide if she liked it or not.

The smuggler leaned over. "What do you think?"

She wrinkled her nose. He laughed and pulled out his flask. "The Germans swear by their beer, but I'll take a Russian vodka any day."

Gerta came back to the table. "Who's ready for the first bath?"

~

FRESH AND CLEAN for the first time in ages, Ruth sank into the warm horsehair bed. Ester lay next to her, her hair tickling Ruth's face. For the first time in weeks, Ruth felt at peace. Safe. It almost felt unreal. For so long she'd thought only of survival, of getting through the day and staying alive. But tomorrow they'd be setting sail for America. She'd be reunited with Tatty and Abraham in less than two weeks.

What would that even be like? Part of her had almost given up on ever seeing them again. She yawned and sank into the deep oblivion of sleep.

Ruth woke the next morning to pin pricks of light through the gauzy curtain. Ester and Momme were already gone. What time was it? She jumped to her feet and found her clothes freshly laundered and folded next to the bed. Gerta was a miracle!

She dressed, washed her face and braided her hair. Climbing down the stairs, she heard the clink of forks on plates and the murmuring of voices. She stopped when she heard the smuggler's throaty chuckle. She was actually going to miss that sound. How lucky they'd been with him.

She remembered the fear and wariness she'd felt in the tavern. If she were Tatty, she'd be offering prayers of thanks for God's intervention. And perhaps, she did believe in a force at work, guiding her to safety in the smuggler's care. But she wasn't quite ready to forgive all her questions of God's judgement these past four years.

She joined everyone at the table for breakfast—the last

moments of calm before the final leg of their journey. She had no idea what to expect of the sea voyage. But she doubted it would include anything like Gerta's cooking and nurturing care.

The smuggler finally stubbed out his cigarette and got to his feet. "It's time."

The women stood and gathered their belongings, Momme rechecking the tucked folds on their bundles one last time.

Gerta met Ruth by the door and offered her a sack of food. "To keep your strength up. There are some ginger cookies to keep the seasickness away."

Ruth smiled and gathered the kind woman in a hug.

The port turned out to be only a short walk from Gerta's inn. The ship's gigantic black hull loomed over the dock, its bright yellow smokestacks spewing smoke against the bright blue sky. The name S.S. Batavia was scrawled across the side in a looping script.

The smuggler reached into his coat pocket and pulled out three tickets. Ruth was surprised by a sudden jolt of fear —a drop in her stomach that made her regret eating that heavy breakfast. They would soon be boarding that ship, joining the slew of ants running to and fro on the deck. There would be nothing but water beneath her, and only an unknown land ahead.

Momme and Ester took their tickets and moved away toward the boat. Ruth stood looking at the ticket in the smuggler's hand. Finally she reached to take it.

"Thank you," she said. "For everything."

He nodded. She turned away to join Momme and Ester, but then stopped and turned back to face him.

"Can you tell me now? Your name?"

He grinned. "Dmitri."

She smiled. "*A sheynem dank,* Dmitri."

It was strange to consider the arbitrariness of life — how this man had changed the entire course of her life, yet now they were parting never to meet again.

How many times had he done this? Would he ever think of her again, hunched over his vodka, smoking his cigarette, or did his mind just shed the memories of each journey and the anguish he had witnessed? How much would she think of *him* when surrounded by the newness of America? Perhaps he would be only a shadowy figure in her dreams—nightmares—recalling this time.

Momme and Ester waited for her by the gangplank. The three of them climbed it together and gave their tickets to the sailor standing at the top. He directed them to their quarters below-deck, but Momme led them instead to the bow of the ship to watch the castoff.

"Need to see us leave it behind?" Ester asked. "Say goodbye?"

Momme shook her head. "No, I want to see us sail ahead. Time to start fresh, my *sheifeles.*"

She put her arms around Ruth and Ester and pulled them to her. Ruth snuggled in to Momme's embrace. They had made it. She finally exhaled the tension she'd been holding, along with all the cynicism, distrust, and survival skills. She could almost feel Jeremiah with them, commending her for trusting her instincts to get them here and reminding her of her strength.

There would always be ugliness in the world, but there was also good. Their journey with the smuggler proved that. And as she stood with Momme and Ester, she was reminded of how much they'd overcome together. Yes, she was strong, but she'd learned she didn't need to shoulder her burdens alone.

The ship rocked beneath her as it pulled from shore. She felt Ester and Momme's locked arms tighten around her. Together they stood, watching as the land dropped away and got smaller and smaller. Until there was nothing but water surrounding them. Only then did they finally turn away and move to find their berth downstairs. It was time to start anew.

The End

Historical Notes

Events Leading to Bloody Sunday

Russia emancipated the serfs in 1870, creating a new peasant working class. However, this brought a new set of problems for the Russian economy and social system. In a system that had always favored the upper class—this was not going to easily change.

Strikes became a popular way to demonstrate discontent with employers and working conditions. However, the Russian term for strikes, *stachka*, was derived from the term, *stakat'sia*, which meant plotting for a criminal act. Strikes were therefore treated as such under the law and viewed as potential acts of rebellion. Despite this, they remained the only tool in the worker's arsenal and as frustration grew, versions of unions and organized efforts began to form.

The most popular was a group called *The Assembly of Russian Factory and Mill Workers of the City of St. Petersburg*-otherwise known as *The Assembly*. This group was headed by a priest named, Father Georgy Gapon. He had inspirational ideas about a Russia with a more equitable social system. He acted on his vision by taking an interest in the unfair plight of the Russian working class and helping them organize without violence. His goal was to evoke change without the government misconstruing their efforts as acts of rebellion.

In December 1904, six workers of the Putilov Ironworks factory in St. Petersburg were fired for their suspected association with the Assembly. In protest, the entire rest of the factory staff walked out. Sympathy strikes across the city occurred as well, bringing up the total number of striking workers to about 150,000 in over 300 factories.

Bloody Sunday

Under Father Gapon's leadership, the striking workers decided to draft a petition and present it to the czar at his palace in a peaceful march on January 22nd, 1905. This decision was made based on established Russian tradition dating back to the 15th century, where individual and group petitions were deemed an appropriate way to bring grievances to the czar from the public.

Gapon drafted the petition himself and included a respectful list of demands for safer working conditions, a reduction of hours, and fairer wages.

The march to the Winter Palace was in no way rebellious, although it was done without the permission of police and the government. Father Gapon forbid any political signage or threatening language. Gapon had even sent a copy of the petition to the Palace ahead of time to pave the way for their peaceful intentions.

Despite these efforts, the day became known forever in

history as Bloody Sunday, with soldiers opening fire on the unarmed crowd. Reports of casualties from the day conflict depending on sources and political leanings. The czar and government reported 96 dead and 300 injured, whereas other sources claim over 1,000 dead and wounded.

Father Gapon's Assembly was shut down that day and he was forced to flee Russia.

Consequences of Bloody Sunday

Although, Czar Nicholas II did not personally order the shots fired, he was blamed for them. Such cold-hearted killing of so many people, left a new bitterness and distrust against the czar and his totalitarian rule.

The Bloody Sunday massacre has been marked as the inciting moment for the later Russian Revolution, as this was the event that turned the tide of working class support against the czar.

As depicted in Ruth's story, from January 1905 forward, Russia descended further and further into chaos and violence with mass strikes and protests erupting across the country.

The Pale of Settlement and Russian Jewish History

The Pale of Settlement was a western part of the Russian Empire that existed from 1791 to 1917. Catherine the Great created it in an effort to speed colonization of the newly acquired Black Sea region. Jews were allowed to increase the land allotted to them, but in exchange, Jewish merchants could no longer conduct business outside the Settlement.

Until then, the Jewish population in Russia had been very limited. It remained that way until the acquisition of the Polish-Lithuanian territory in 1793, which substantially increased the Jewish population.

At its height the Pale of Settlement had a population of over 500 million and represented the bulk of the world's Jewish population. As a result of the overpopulation of such a limited area, most residents were quite poor without enough jobs or resources to support them.

The name, the Pale of Settlement, arose under Nicholas I's rule. During his reign, he shrank the area of the settlement and also put more restrictions into place. He tried to resettle *all* the Jews living in acquired territories and cities throughout the Russian Empire to the Pale. However, this soon became difficult to enforce, and over time the restrictions lessened again.

Things looked up under Alexander II's rule during the mid to late 1800s. He expanded the rights of rich and educated Jews, allowing them to return to areas outside the Settlement. People began to hope the Pale of Settlement might even be abolished. These hopes vanished when Alexander II was assassinated in 1881. Rumors spread that he was killed by a Jew and anti-sentiment against Jews skyrocketed.

Amongst this clamp down of rights and rising persecution, many residents of the Settlement immigrated to the United States. But even the rate of emigration could not keep up with the steady number of Jews expelled from other areas of Russia and the Pale of Settlement remained overpopulated and strained economically.

World War I finally marked the end of Russia's hold on the Jewish population. With Germany's invasion, Jews were forced to flee the Settlement into other parts of Russia. By

August of 1915, the boundaries of the Pale of Settlement were unenforceable. The Pale formally came to an end with the abdication of Nicholas II and the Russian Revolution. In 1917, the new Provisional Government officially abolished the Pale of Settlement.

Review Request

Did you enjoy reading this book? If so, could you please post a review?

Goodreads and bookstores rank books by sales as well as reviews. So, every review counts and would make a world of difference for this Indie Author. Thank you! Thank you! And please just click below!

Leave your Goodreads Review Here!

Also by Joyana Peters

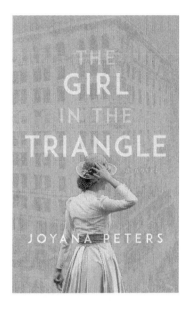

The Girl in the Triangle

Are you an Author looking to Publish?

The world of self and Indie Publishing can feel overwhelming and intimidating to navigate. But fear not, you're not alone, and it doesn't need to feel intimidating.

I offer courses and coaching opportunities on my website at JoyanaPeters.com. I even offer a free fifteen minute call to discuss exactly where you are and your needs for your self-publishing journey. Book a FREE call today!

Would you like a free short story? Sign up for my newsletter at JoyanaPeters.com and get your free short story about the Triangle Shirtwaist Factory Fire!

Join my newsletter and get your free short story here!

Would you like to make sure you are the first to hear about my new releases and book promos? Follow me on Bookbub and Goodreads!

Follow me on Bookbub
Follow me on Goodreads

About the Author

Joyana Peters is the author of the best-selling novel, *The Girl in the Triangle*. She's won a number of awards including—the SCBWI YA Spark Award, IBPA's Ben Franklin Award for Historical Fiction, and the Book Excellence Award for Multicultural Fiction. She was also a Top Five Finalist for *Shelf Unbound's* Indie Best Book of the Year.

Joyana got her MFA in Creative Writing from the University of New Orleans. She taught composition on both the secondary and university levels. She also writes non-fiction and has been published in publications nationwide.

Joyana lives in Northern Virginia with her two kids, husband, and goofy yellow lab, Gatsby.

facebook.com/JoyanaPetersAuthor

instagram.com/joyanapetersauthor

bookbub.com/profile/joyana-peters

Acknowledgments

They say it takes a village and that is true even in book writing. There's the illusion of the solitary author slaving away in isolation to write a book. And although that is the case when it comes to getting the actual words on paper, that discounts the many people who support the author emotionally along the way.

In my case, I've been blessed with **_many_** supportive individuals in my village.

To my parents—Thank you for coming along this ride with me. You've celebrated every part of _The Girl in the Triangle's_ success with me, helped pick me up from my falls, and pushed me to keep going on the next book. This has truly been a dream come true and I'm so grateful to share all this joy with the people who believed in me from the start.

To my sister—Thank you for continuing to be my voice of reason and for continuing to guide me in finding my balance and true meaning of success.

To my in-laws—Thank you for always being in my corner. I am forever grateful for your thoughtful curation of resources, your opinions on design, proofreading help, and support along the way.

To my writing group—Once again, you've been integral to this process. You saw these pages from start to finish and helped me carve out these characters and find their story. I am forever grateful to you all and I continue to be a better writer because of you!

To my friends and extended family--You're been the best cheerleaders and Street Team a girl could ask for! Thank you for remembering to ask how the book was coming and letting me blab about plotting and characters and the crazy writing process. I am also so grateful to you for continuing to share *The Girl in the Triangle* with your friends and families. You always have my back and I love you for it!

To my children--My beautiful babies, it has been amazing to share this with you. I love that you both tell everyone you meet that your mommy is a writer. I love that you know the names of these books and ask about them regularly. I hope I can continue to model living out a dream for you and inspire you to do the same! Spread your wings and reach for the stars, my little ones!

To my amazing husband--My love, my life. You had no idea what you were getting into when you married me. But man, have you risen to the challenge! You've supported me in ways I couldn't even have dreamed and been my rock through it all. Thank you for always believing in me, even when you think I'm crazy!

Enjoy a Sneak Peek of Joyana's Next Book!

Clara: The Girl Behind an Uprising is Joyana's new work in progress! Enjoy this sneak peek of the first chapter here. To enjoy more sneak peek chapters you can join Joyana's new VIP group on her website-JoyanaPeters.com. VIP members get access to works in progress content, her history talk video replays and additional bonus content.

Clara: The Girl Behind an Uprising

Chapter One

Clara Lemlich stood on the stage looking down at the sea of expectant garment workers before her. Feeling slightly dizzy, she wished she had a podium to steady herself. Was she really doing this? Calling a strike?

Only moments before, she'd *been* one of the crowd of disgruntled workers sitting down below. But something had snapped inside her. She'd felt so hot she might explode. The union leaders just wanted to talk endlessly—they didn't seem to care if anything actually *changed*. In fact, they seemed more concerned about placating the garment factory owners instead of the workers they were meant to serve! How dare they!

The, next thing she knew, she was stomping across the stage, drawing the crowd's electric attention like a lightning rod. "I've got something to say!"

It grew quiet. Dead silent. Clara swallowed nervously. Now what? She groped for her grandmother's gold locket that hung around her neck. Reflexively, her thumb rubbed the smooth metal. As usual, it steadied her. Helped clear her head.

"I've listened to all these words. My patience is gone for words. I move we go on strike!"

The crowd erupted with cheers before her.

She gestured for quiet again. "If you're with me, repeat after me!"

She took a deep breath and recited the words aloud from the Jewish oath of fidelity. She shivered as the garment workers, mostly girls, repeated it with her, binding them all to the cause. As the oath drew to a close, she nodded and turned to the men standing behind her.

The nearest union leader crossed his arms and scowled. "You have no idea what you've done," he whispered.

She responded, making sure her voice carried to every corner of the room. "I leave you to inform the garment factory owners the garment workers are on strike."

Chaos unfolded as girls jumped to their feet. A swirl of chatter and exclamations surrounded Clara as she descended to the floor below. A few girls patted her on the back with words of congratulations, but she scanned the crowd looking for the only two people she needed to see. She glimpsed them pushing their way through to her.

Pauline Newman stood with her hands on her hips and

Rose Schneiderman shook her head and smiled. "Well, you certainly know how to make a statement."

Clara ran to them and grabbed them by the arms. "I don't know what got into me."

Pauline softened. "You did what we all wanted. Just no one else was brave enough."

They squeezed hands. Clara took in the jubilant faces around her. The shouts of excitement. Pauline was right, she had spoken the true feelings of the masses. Whatever happened, she'd done *that*, at least.

"So, what now?" Rose asked.

Clara's chest tightened. "I have no idea."

Clara looked to Pauline's pursed lips. She knew what Pauline was thinking, why she'd stood there with her hands on her hips. Clara had been reckless, had spoken without a plan. But what an opportunity! She didn't regret grabbing it. She just hoped she wouldn't be alone in shouldering the responsibility of whatever came next.

Pauline sighed. "We have a long night ahead of us. Come."

Clara grinned. It would be okay. She'd taken a massive risk, most definitely. One that would impact *many* women who were now depending on her. But she had her best friends by her side to help her.

Made in the USA
Middletown, DE
25 August 2023